THE HORSESHOE TRILOGIES

In Good Faith

Read all the books in the first set of
Horseshoe Trilogies:

Book #1: Keeping Faith
Book #2: Last Hope
Book #3: Sweet Charity

And in the second set of trilogies:
Book #4: In Good Faith

COMING SOON:

Book #5: Where There's Hope

THE HORSESHOE TRILOGIES

In Good Faith

by
Lucy Daniels

VOLO
HYPERION
New York

Special thanks to Michelle Bates
Thanks also to Luisa Smith, B.V.M.S., M.R.C.V.S., for reviewing
the veterinary material contained in this book.

Text copyright © 2003 by Working Partners Limited
Illustrations copyright © 2003 by Tristan Elwell

First published in England by Hodder Children's Books under the series title
Perfect Ponies.

The Horseshoe Trilogies, Volo, and the Volo colophon are trademarks of
Disney Enterprises, Inc.

First U.S. edition, 2003
1 3 5 7 9 10 8 6 4 2

This book is set in 12.5-point Life Roman.
ISBN 0-7868-1747-X
Visit www.volobooks.com

For Vera—for teaching me all there is to know
about Faith, Hope, and Charity

In Good Faith

CHAPTER ONE

"I think we're going to be happy here, Rascal," Josie Grace said, bending down to tickle the tummy of her little black-and-white cat. Rascal rolled over, stretching in the warm afternoon sun that was streaming in through the bedroom window.

Josie stood up and looked around her room. She had made good progress with the unpacking, but there was still so much to do. Boxes and crates were piled high and clothes and books spilled out of suitcases. She picked up the little silver photo frame on her bedside table. Three horses stared out at her—three very special horses—Faith, Hope, and Charity. Tucking a stray auburn curl behind her ear,

Josie smiled and put the photo back where it belonged. This might not be School Farm, the riding stables where she had lived all of her life, but this new house was starting to feel like home.

Through the tangled wilderness at the back of the garden, Josie could see the field that was home to one of those horses, Charity. The mare was standing by the gate, her silvery gray coat shimmering in the sunlight. She was a beautiful horse—gray from top to toe, except for the pale blaze running down her face, and her white mane and tail. At least Josie had been able to take Charity with her when she moved. And Faith and Hope, the other School Farm riding horses, had gone to good homes. Josie and her parents had made sure of that.

"It's too hot to be unpacking," Josie muttered under her breath as she watched Charity begin to canter across the grass. Josie hesitated, then turned and made her way down the steep spiral staircase. "Mom," she called. "Where are you?"

"In here," a voice came from the floor below. Josie ran the rest of the way down into the kitchen. Her mother was standing with a cup and saucer in her hands, a puzzled look on her face.

"I'd forgotten we had these," said Mary Grace, putting the dishes down on the table. "So, how are you doing? All unpacked?"

"Um, not exactly," Josie said. "But I'm getting there, and I was wondering . . ."

"Ye-es?" Mrs. Grace raised her eyebrows.

"Well, I've unpacked some of my clothes and I've put my posters on the wall and . . ."

"Go on, then." Mrs. Grace smiled, her gray eyes dancing. "Take Charity out for a ride."

"Thanks, Mom." Josie grinned. She dashed out of the room and back up the stairs. "I'm going to ride over to see Faith and Jill," she called.

Jill Atterbury was Faith's new owner. She lived on the other side of Littlehaven, which made it close enough for Josie to visit. Josie hurried back down the stairs in jodhpurs and a T-shirt and grabbed her riding hat.

"Just make sure you're back in time for dinner," her mother's voice trailed after Josie's retreating figure. "Dad's cooking. . . ."

Josie hurried across the yard and into the shed. She grabbed a handful of treats, then picked up Charity's bridle and slung it over her shoulder before collecting the saddle. She made her way down the dirt path and approached the field. "Charity!" she called.

Charity raised her head from where she was grazing on the other side of the field and whinnied loudly. Josie felt a rush of happiness as the horse trotted across the grass toward her.

When she reached her, Charity nuzzled Josie's hand, knowing that she would find a treat there. Josie opened her hand and fed the gray mare a small mint. Quickly, she ran a body brush over Charity's coat to get rid of the dust, then reached up to slide the bridle over Charity's head. Charity stood patiently as Josie put the saddle on her back and buckled the girth. "Now we're ready," she declared.

The sun was high in the sky as they set off through the back of the field. Gently, they meandered down the bridle paths in the direction of Jill's house on the other side of Littlehaven. The bushes were covered with little white flowers and the air smelled sweet as they trotted along. When they were out in open fields again, Josie urged Charity into a canter and soon they reached the gate that led to the road to Jill's house. The Atterburys lived in a modern housing development, but they were surrounded on all sides by green fields.

Josie and Charity walked along the grassy path, the smell of the countryside enveloping them. Soon they were turning up the driveway that ran alongside Jill's house. As they reached the field where Faith now lived, Josie could see Jill, standing with Faith. Josie halted Charity for a moment. Jill looked completely happy, and Faith's bay coat shone like polished leather in the afternoon sun.

As horse and girl stood nose-to-nose in the field, Josie felt a lump in her throat. Two months ago she had been the one looking after Faith. She stopped herself. When her family had been forced to leave their riding school, they'd had no choice but to look for a new home for Faith, and Faith was happy here with Jill.

Charity let out a loud whinny of recognition and Jill looked around and waved.

"Hey, Jill," Josie called, waving back as she walked Charity forward. Faith nickered softly as Josie undid the gate and walked through. As Charity drew level with Faith, the two horses snuffled each other affectionately.

"So how are you doing?" Josie asked, jumping down from Charity's back.

"Great, and you're just in time," Jill said, smiling. "I was about to give Faith a little bath."

"Well, I'll let Charity go in the field, and then I'll help you," said Josie as Faith stamped her foreleg impatiently.

"All right, all right, Faith," said Jill. She turned back to face Josie. "You've just missed Bev," she went on. "She exercised Faith for me today." A gentle breeze rippled through the trees, ruffling her shoulder-length brown hair. Jill looked sad, and Josie felt awful. Jill was so much better now—all that was left as a reminder of the car accident she'd been in was a slight limp. But she had been forced to give up riding and sell her horse, Marmalade. When her parents had seen how unhappy she was, they'd bought Faith, because recently the gentle bay mare needed more love and affection than riding, which Jill was happy to give.

"I'm going to see the specialist tomorrow," Jill said. "He's going to tell me if I can ride again."

"So your hip's getting better?" Josie asked as she started to untack Faith.

"Seems so," Jill replied. "The specialist is pleased with my progress. All those exercises I've been doing have paid off." She bent down and put her head through her legs in a mock demonstration.

"Oh, Jill," Josie said, grinning. "That's not a real exercise, is it?"

"Not exactly," Jill admitted, laughing. "But it made you smile." Then a cloud seemed to pass across Jill's eyes, darkening her thin, pale face. "Even if I am able to ride, it's going to have to be sidesaddle," she said, untangling a knot from Faith's mane. "The specialist has said that it'll place less pressure on my hip."

"Well, that's okay, isn't it?" Josie said.

"I suppose so," Jill replied, nodding. "I'm just worried that it won't be very easy or fun."

"Oh, I'm sure you'll pick it up soon enough," Josie said confidently. "Faith's got such a broad back, she's perfect for riding sidesaddle, and she's got such an easygoing temperament. And I'll be here to help you too, of course."

"Really?" said Jill, looking relieved. "I'd love it if we could ride together."

"So would I," Josie grinned.

The two girls started sponging Faith down in a comfortable silence. Soon they had removed the grass stains from her coat and Josie bent down to wash Faith's four white "socks"—the white bottom part of the horse's legs.

"So how's Hope?" asked Jill.

"She's very happy," Josie replied. Hope was Charity's mother—a gray mare, and one of the gentlest horses around. She was at a new home, Friendship House—a center for physically challenged children—where she was dearly loved.

"Well, I'm glad to hear she's okay," said Jill as Josie bent down and ran her hand down Faith's near foreleg.

"Come on, Faith, up," said Josie.

Obediently, the mare lifted her leg and Josie bent down to pick out her hoof. Gently she ran a hoof-pick around the inside of the horseshoe. Then she put Faith's foot back on the ground and the two girls took turns picking out the other three. When they were finished, they leaned against the stall wall.

"I think we've earned a rest," said Jill, wiping a hand across her forehead. "Why don't we let Faith join Charity? Then we could go inside and grab a cold drink. I could show you the sidesaddle my mom and dad bought," she added.

"Great!" Josie replied.

Josie watched as Jill undid Faith's halter and let the mare off into the field. Faith walked a few steps before she dropped to the ground and began to joyfully roll in the dirt.

"Typical!" Jill groaned, rolling her eyes. "All that hard work for nothing. Figures that Faith would already get dirty. Come on, Josie. Let's go and get a snack."

The two girls ran up the path to the modern redbrick house. The garage was right next to it. Jill pressed a button on the wall that raised the door. "There it is," she said, pointing. "Ready and waiting."

Josie screwed up her eyes to adjust to the light, and then she saw it—a beautiful leather saddle resting on a stand at the back of the garage. "Wow!" she said, walking over and running her hands over the soft, tanned leather. It looked different from the saddle she used because it had two pommels and only one stirrup, hanging down the left-hand side.

"It's secondhand, of course," said Jill. "There aren't many people that make them anymore. This one's about fifty years old, but it fits Faith perfectly. A saddler came out to make sure of that."

"It's wonderful," Josie said.

"What's wonderful?" The door at the side of the garage opened, and a tall man with a kind face joined them.

"Oh, hi, Dad," said Jill. "I was just showing Josie my new saddle."

"Isn't it great?" Mr. Atterbury said, putting an arm around his daughter's shoulder. "We're happy it's going to allow Jill to ride again." After he gave Jill a hug, Mr. Atterbury turned to Josie. "So how's the new house? Have you settled in yet?"

"It's great," Josie said. "My room's on the top floor and there's even a yard, so we've been able to bring all the ducks and chickens with us from School Farm. We haven't got a pond for them yet, but Dad's going to work on that."

"It sounds as though he's got his work cut out for him!" Mr. Atterbury laughed. "Of course, the good thing for us is that you're just down the street, so you can come and see Faith whenever you want. I know Jill loves having you here."

"Oh, Dad, you're not going to get all sappy on us, are you?" said Jill, looking embarrassed. "Come on, Josie. Time for that cold drink."

The two girls chose a couple of cans from the fridge and drank them thirstily.

Josie glanced at her watch. "Yikes! I said I'd be home for dinner in fifteen minutes," she said. "I'll have to fly. Bye, Mr. Atterbury!"

The two girls hurried down the path and found Faith and Charity grazing in the middle of the field. At the sound of the girls' approach, the two horses looked up.

"Time to go home, Charity," Josie called. She walked into the middle of the field and coaxed Charity over. Then she brought her over to the fence to tack her up. She finished tightening the girth, put her foot in the stirrup, and swung herself onto Charity's back.

As she gathered up the reins, Faith let out a little whinny, which tugged on Josie's heartstrings. It still hurt to have to say good-bye to her, but each time it was a little easier than the last. And it made it a whole lot better for her, knowing that Faith liked her new home and that she could come visit.

"Bye, Jill." Josie waved and took one last look at Faith. "I can see that Faith's going to be happy here," she whispered to her horse. "Really happy."

CHAPTER TWO

"Mom . . . Dad . . . I'm back. . . ." Josie called, pushing back the door to the house. The warm, inviting smell of tomato sauce greeted her. "Hello, Basil," she said, almost tripping over the terrier who lay stretched across the hallway.

Josie walked into the kitchen, where she found her father stirring a pan on the stove.

"Try this," he said. He held out a wooden spoon of the sauce. "What do you think? Does it need a little more salt?"

"Definitely," Josie answered. "So, where's Mom?" she asked.

"Over here," a voice called. "I've just finished

unpacking the boxes in the living room," said Mary Grace as she came into the kitchen.

"I think that calls for a celebration," Robert Grace announced. "And I have just the thing," he said, holding up the saucepan.

Josie and her mom laughed.

"Can you set the table please, Josie?" asked her father. "We've got some guests joining us for dinner."

"Guests?" Josie said, puzzled. "The last time we had *guests* it was your teacher friends. And you talked school stuff all evening."

"Well, you'll just have to wait and find out who it is this time," Josie's dad said with a twinkle in his eye. "It's a surprise."

Josie frowned. "I'm not that big on surprises," she said warily.

"Oh, I don't know, the last one wasn't so bad, was it?" her mother teased.

Josie grinned. Her mother was referring to Charity, of course. Josie had been the last one to know they were going to be able to keep her. They'd been looking for weeks for an owner, not really wanting to part with her. Then, when her father got a raise at school, keeping her had become a reality. Josie's parents had managed to keep it a surprise until the very last minute.

"So?" Josie said, looking at her dad. But Mr. Grace just raised his eyebrows and continued cooking. Josie sighed and walked over to a drawer to gather up the silverware.

"Can you bring the chickens and ducks in and give them their evening feed when you've finished that?" Josie's mother asked.

"Sure," Josie replied. Putting the last spoon into place, she left the kitchen and made her way to the shed. There she grabbed a handful of grain from the sacks, placed it in a bucket, and walked back outside.

"Where are you?" she called, rattling the pail. There was a squawking noise and a flurry of eager faces appeared from the undergrowth. "I didn't think you'd stay hidden for long," Josie said, coaxing them over to the little wooden henhouse on the edge of the lawn.

Once the hens and ducks were safely inside and busy enjoying their supper, Josie turned to go. "Sleep tight," she said.

As she began to walk back up the garden path, she heard the front doorbell ring. "Wonder who this is?" she murmured to herself. She pulled down the handle and pushed open the back door.

"Surprise!" a volley of voices greeted her.

"Anna! Ben! What are you doing here?" Josie grinned. Anna Marshall was Josie's best friend from school, and Ben was her twin brother. "I wasn't expecting you back until Monday."

"Well we couldn't keep away from you," Anna joked. "Actually, Dad brought us back a little early. He had to go on a business trip unexpectedly."

Anna and Ben's parents were separated. They lived with their mother in the neighboring town, but they often went to visit their father in the city.

"And I thought I'd join you too," came a voice, as Anna and Ben's mother, Lynne, walked into the kitchen. She waved at Josie, making the silver bracelets on her wrist jangle.

"Well, I think we're ready," said Robert Grace. "Let's sit down and eat."

"Good idea, I'm starving," said Anna, pulling back a chair next to Josie.

"So what's new?" Josie asked, passing plates of steaming pasta around the table.

"I went to see Tubber today," said Ben.

"How was he?" Mrs. Grace asked.

"He was very good," Ben replied, grinning.

Tubber was one of the horses that had been kept at School Farm. He was owned by Mary Collins, a teacher at Josie's father's school. Ben had always exercised him, and when Tubber had moved, Ben had continued with the arrangement. The pair were devoted to each other.

"Ben has to bike to the other side of Littlehaven each day," Anna added. "But I think he'd bike twenty miles if it meant seeing that horse. Oh, and we start back at Lonsdale on Saturday. Those are the stables we've been riding at," she explained.

"Tell the Graces about the fair," Lynne said.

Anna grinned. "Lonsdale is putting on a fair in two weeks to raise money for Friendship House."

"We're taking part as well," Lynne added. Lynne was an art teacher at Friendship House. "You should see how excited the kids are. Hope's going to be pulling a cart and I'm going to be making all the costumes."

"That's great," Josie said.

"Our Hope, the center of attention." Mary Grace beamed. "How exciting."

"Any money that's raised is going to the Friendship House Charity Fund," Lynne explained.

"So what sort of a fair is it?" asked Mr. Grace.

"A medieval one," Anna said. "Everyone gets to dress up in costume—even the horses."

"There's even going to be a gymkhana with games like spear ringing and pole bending," Ben announced through a mouthful of pasta.

"Well, it sounds wonderful," said Mrs. Grace.

"It would be great if you would get involved too," Lynne said. "They're looking for more volunteers."

"I could ride Charity," Josie said.

"And I could ride Connie," Mrs. Grace said. Connie was the black mare she exercised for her friend in a nearby town.

"Well, I won't be riding, so maybe I could help out with the stalls," Mr. Grace said. "I could rent some stocks—you know, to put people in so you can throw sponges at them!"

"That's a good idea," agreed Lynne. "I'll see what they think about that at Lonsdale."

"We're going to Friendship House tomorrow to help out," Anna said to Josie. "Why don't you come along?" she suggested. "You could see Hope."

"That sounds great," Josie said. "What time are you meeting up?"

"Ten," said Anna.

"Ten it is, then." Josie grinned. This surprise guest dinner was turning about better than she had thought!

Once the table was cleared and the dishwasher loaded, the Marshalls went home and Mr. Grace disappeared off to his study. Josie and her mom had a few moments alone.

"The medieval fair sounds like a great idea," her mom said.

"It does, doesn't it?" Josie said. "I wonder if Jill and Faith would like to be involved too."

"What a good idea," said Mrs. Grace. "How was Jill today?"

"She was okay," said Josie. "She's going to the specialist tomorrow to see if she can ride. She's got to start all over again and learn sidesaddle."

"Sidesaddle?" Mrs. Grace echoed. "I never

learned how to teach that," she said, looking thoughtful.

Josie knew her words had brought back memories for her mother of School Farm and all the students she had taught there. She'd had to give it up when they'd moved away. She gave her mother a hug. "Don't be sad," she said.

Josie's mom nodded and gave her daughter a hug back. "I'll try, and it is getting easier now that we have settled here. I know it hasn't been easy for you either, leaving School Farm and losing the horses, especially Faith—she was very special to us."

Josie nodded, feeling upset for a moment as she thought of the bay mare. Then she brightened up. "Do you remember the time we put the feeding back an hour and Faith sulked for days?" she asked.

Her mother smiled. "And what about the time Charity learned to open the door of her stall and we found her trotting around the yard?"

"We had to fix the bolt pretty fast." Josie said.

It felt good to talk about their previous lives at School Farm. Slowly it was starting to feel less painful, and the happy memories were coming back. "I'm just going to say good-night to Charity," Josie said.

"All right, but it's bedtime, so don't be too long," replied her mother.

Josie nodded and, grabbing a light sweater, headed for the door. She let herself out and ran down to the little path at the end of the yard. It was starting to get dark outside and the fragrance of summer flowers lingered in the air. A familiar whinny greeted her. Josie felt a wave of contentment flood through her.

"Hi, Charity," she called. There was a flash of mane and tail, and the gray mare appeared on the other side of the fence. Josie patted her smooth neck. "How are you, my girl?" she said, fumbling in her pocket for a peppermint as the horse snuffled at her sweater. "You can still smell Faith on me, can't you?" Josie said. Charity's ears flicked back and forth and her eyes slowly closed. Josie tickled her nose. "I don't believe you're listening to a word I'm saying, are you?" she crooned.

The horse leaned her head on Josie's shoulder. Josie smiled and stepped out from under Charity's head. She started to walk back up the path to the house. When she had gone a little way, she took one last look back at her horse. Charity had already ambled away and was grazing. The moon had come out from behind a cloud, lighting up Charity's silvery coat. Josie let out a peaceful sigh. Everything was working out much better than she had expected.

CHAPTER THREE

"How was Friendship House?" Mr. Grace called out as Josie opened the little gate to their yard the following afternoon.

"It was fun," Josie replied, walking into the garden. She had been there for a couple of hours and Anna and Ben had been right—everyone was really excited about the fair, and their enthusiasm had been infectious. And then there had been Hope. . . . the little gray horse looked so happy and loved. "Actually, it was better than good," Josie went on. "It was great. So what's this you're digging?" she asked, pointing to a large hole.

"Well, I finally got the go-ahead for that duck

pond," her dad said. "Mr. Brown has said it's all right."

Mr. Brown was the landlord of their house, so they had to get his permission for any changes they made.

"We should have had the good sense to leave the ducks behind if you ask me," Mr. Grace grumbled.

"Oh, Dad, you don't mean that." Josie said. "You like them as much as Mom and I do."

"Yes, well I'd like them even more if I didn't have to do this!" said Mr. Grace, leaning on his spade and rubbing his forehead. "And there I was thinking the summer break was going to be a vacation!"

"Two more shovelfuls, Dad," said Josie. "How about I make you a snack?"

Mr. Grace nodded appreciatively. "Thanks, sweetheart."

Josie turned and walked down the garden path toward the house, just as the telephone rang. She ran inside to answer it. "Hello," she said.

"Hello, Josie."

"Jill!" Josie cried. "How are you?"

"I'm fine," replied Jill. "I've just got back from the specialist."

"So?" Josie asked. "How did it go? What did the doctor say?"

"Well, it's good news," said Jill. "My hip's getting much better, and all of the exercises have been working. . . ." Her words tumbled out one after another in her excitement.

"And?" Josie asked.

"He said that I'm fit," Jill burst out. "I can start to ride again!"

"That's fantastic news!" Josie exclaimed. "When are you going to start?"

"Well, there's no time like the present," said Jill. "Why don't you come on over?"

"I've told Mom and Dad that I don't want them to get involved," Jill said as she opened the front door of the house, already dressed in her jodhpurs and riding boots. "This is something I want to do without them. I told them you'd offered to help me," she added, leading Josie inside.

"But aren't we going to need some help with the sidesaddle?" Josie asked. "I've never fitted one before."

"Oh, don't worry about that," said Jill. "The

saddler who delivered the saddle showed me what to do, and he gave me a quick riding demonstration, too. I'm sure we'll work it out. Come on, I'm going to need a hand lifting it. It weighs a ton."

Jill grabbed her riding hat, then she and Josie walked into the garage.

"You were right when you said it was heavy," Josie gasped as she tried to lift the saddle.

"It weighs more than a normal saddle," Jill agreed. "It'll be easier if we carry it together."

Josie walked around to the pommel and Jill took the cantle at the back. Between them, they managed to lug the saddle out of the garage.

"You will be careful, won't you?" Mrs. Atterbury said from the kitchen.

"I'm not a baby, Mom," Jill said. "I *can* ride."

"I know you can," said Mrs. Atterbury, looking a little hurt. "It's just that it's been a while."

"Don't worry. I'll be fine!" Jill said, giving her mother a quick wave. "Can you grab that, please, Josie?" she asked, pointing to a book on sidesaddle riding that was lying on the kitchen table.

Josie and Jill made their way down the garden. When they reached the field, they rested the heavy saddle on the fence. There wasn't a cloud in the sky as the two girls walked across the grass. Jill held out a handful of grain, the halter slung over her shoulder, and Faith walked over. Jill slipped the halter on Faith's head and led her back to the fence.

"Shall I go and get a body brush?" Josie said.

"That would be great," Jill answered.

Josie hurried off to the stable to pick up the grooming kit and brought it back out. Jill was just placing the reins of the bridle over Faith's neck when Josie returned. "There we are," Josie said, giving Faith a quick brush. "Now it's just the saddle. We need to get it up there somehow." Josie looked at Faith a little uncertainly. Faith was 14.3 hands, so it was a fair stretch for something so heavy. Faith snorted and pawed at the ground, as if anxious to get going.

After three attempts, it was clear the girls were going to need more than just two pairs of hands to get the saddle onto Faith's back.

"This is no good," Josie admitted finally. "We can't do this on our own."

"Do you want a hand with that?" a voice called out from behind them.

Josie was relieved to see Mr. Atterbury hurrying down the path toward them. She looked at Jill, who had gone a little quiet.

"I'm not going to interfere," said Mr. Atterbury, having noticed the look on Jill's face. "I'll just lift it up, then I'll leave you alone. There you are," he said, as he placed the saddle on Faith's back.

"Thanks, Dad," said Jill. "We have to start by loosely girthing her," she explained to Josie. Mr. Atterbury waved and walked back to the house.

Josie bent down and buckled the saddle into place. It was different from a usual saddle because there were two girths and a balancing strap that held the saddle securely in place.

"Then we need to run a hand between Faith and the saddle," Jill went on. "We should be able to slide a hand comfortably under all of the points of contact."

"There, it looks fine," said Josie.

Faith blew in and out through her nostrils. Even for the most patient of horses, it was hot standing in the summer sun.

"Ready?" Josie asked Jill.

"I think so," Jill said excitedly.

"Here," Josie said. "You're going to need a leg up. On the count of three, you push up."

"Okay." Jill nodded.

She looked pale and worried, and Josie felt nervous for her friend. All of Jill's hopes of riding rested on this being a success. Josie paused for a moment, then braced herself to lift Jill. "One . . . two . . . three," she said.

Jill tried to jump, but it was obviously hard for her weak hip, and she didn't get very far.

"You need to push a bit more firmly on my hand next time," Josie said.

This time, Jill gave such a large push that she overbalanced and still didn't reach the saddle.

"Okay," Josie said, puffing. "One more time."

This time they were successful, and Jill landed neatly on top. She beamed happily as she bent down to pat Faith's neck. Josie handed Jill the long whip that would take the place of her right leg.

Whew, Josie thought. She jumped up onto the fence and sat in the sun. Then she opened up the book on riding sidesaddle.

"What does it say I should do?" Jill asked.

"Er, you should put your right leg around the top pommel and your left leg under the bottom pommel," Josie read aloud. "Then you put your foot in the stirrup." She closed the book as Jill rearranged her legs and gathered up the reins.

"Maybe start by walking around the field?" Josie suggested, jumping down from the fence.

Jill clicked to Faith, urging her forward, but Faith didn't move. "How do I get her to go?" Jill asked. "I can't use my legs to squeeze."

"You can use your left leg, and give a little tap with the whip," Josie replied.

Jill tried to do as Josie said, but still Faith didn't move. "Nothing's happening," she said in a panicky voice.

"Try again," Josie said. "Try to use your seat. Sit deep in the saddle and ask Faith to go forward with your body."

This seemed to work and soon Faith was walking around the field. She stepped slowly and carefully, unsure about the new weight she was carrying.

This isn't going to be easy, Josie thought. As much as she hated to admit it, she didn't really know what she was doing, and now Jill was grabbing at the reins. "Maybe we should get you a neck strap," Josie called out.

"I don't need one of those," said Jill. "They're for babies. I'm going to try a trot."

Josie had to stop herself from calling out when she saw Jill give Faith a dig in the ribs with her left leg to make her walk faster. It didn't look very comfortable, and now Jill was clutching at the reins even more. "Try and be a bit lighter with your hands," Josie suggested, cringing as she saw Jill accidentally jab Faith in the mouth. "Maybe we should have started on a lunge," she said.

"Well, it's too late for that now," Jill called back a little grumpily.

It clearly wasn't working, and Jill was starting to look very hot and bothered. Josie didn't know what to say as Jill increased Faith's speed without really meaning to. Faith was pushed into a ragged trot as they circled the field. The quicker they got, the more Jill pulled at Faith's mouth. The bay mare's neck was rigid with tension, her eyes rolled miserably, and all the time she was getting faster and faster as Jill communicated her anxiety to the horse.

"Slow her down!" Josie cried, as a red-faced Jill bounced around the field.

"I can't!" Jill gasped, fear written all over her face. "She won't do as I ask."

"Yes, she will," said Josie. "You're just sending her mixed messages. Try to relax the reins and sit up tall."

Jill frowned with concentration as she did what Josie suggested. To Josie's relief, Faith slowed down until she was walking calmly around the field. Josie ran toward them. "Well done," she said. "See, you're fine now."

"That's it," said Jill. "I've had enough. I can't do this. Let me get down."

Josie walked over and helped Jill out of the saddle. Once Jill was on the ground, she turned and buried her face in Faith's mane. "I've forgotten how to ride," she wailed.

"It's not that you've forgotten," said Josie. "It's just that it's a different way of riding. Maybe we should call it a day for now and try again tomorrow."

"All right," Jill sighed. "That's probably a good idea—my hip's aching." She led Faith to the fence where the girls untacked her and gave her a quick rubdown before releasing her into the field. As they carried the sidesaddle back up to the house, Josie wondered what she could say to comfort her friend.

"How did it go?" Jill's mother asked when the girls opened the door to the kitchen.

"Terribly," Jill groaned as her mother walked over and gave her a hug. Her father looked up from a pile of paperwork at the kitchen table and smiled sympathetically. "It was really hard," Jill confessed.

"It's bound to be difficult the first time," said her mother. "It's just going to take practice."

"But it's so different from the way I used to ride," Jill protested.

"What you need are lessons," Josie said. "And I'm not really the best person to help you."

"Well, there's our answer then." Mrs. Atterbury beamed. "We'll get Jill some lessons so she and Faith can learn together." Then she frowned. "School Farm would have been perfect."

Josie tried to disguise the sad look that crossed her face, but it was too late, Mrs. Atterbury had clearly seen it. "I'm sorry for mentioning School Farm, Josie," she said. "I know it's still upsetting for you."

"No, it's okay," Josie said bravely.

Mrs. Atterbury nodded. "I don't suppose your mother would be able to come and tutor Jill, would she?"

"I had thought of that," said Josie. "But she's never taught sidesaddle before."

"Oh dear." Mrs. Atterbury looked thoughtful. "And what about another riding barn? Do you know of any around here?"

"Not really," Josie said.

Jill looked disappointed. Then a thought crossed Josie's mind. "Although there are the stables where Anna rides. Anna's my friend from school," she explained. "She says the stables are great, but the riding school's a little way from here. It's more of a car ride than riding distance."

"That wouldn't be good," Jill said, looking disappointed. "How would I get Faith over there?"

"We haven't got a trailer," Mrs. Atterbury said.

"Well, maybe you could stable Faith there," Josie suggested. "Just for a couple of weeks."

"Oh, I don't think I'd like that," Jill said quickly. "I've gotten so used to having her here."

"But it wouldn't be for long," Josie pointed out.

"Just until you're riding again, then you could bring Faith back home."

"I really can't see any other way, if you want to ride, darling," said Mrs. Atterbury.

"And Lonsdale is supposed to be really nice," said Josie. "In fact, it's putting on a medieval fair in a couple of weeks. I was going to ask you if you wanted to be in it."

"Lonsdale?" Jill questioned, looking concerned. "You're talking about Lonsdale? I couldn't go there."

"Why not?" Josie asked, surprised. "What's wrong with it?"

"We sold Marmalade to Lonsdale," Mrs. Atterbury explained. "Sally, the woman who runs the place, is really nice, but Jill always said she didn't want to see Marmalade in his new home."

"It was hard enough having to let him go," Jill said.

Josie nodded. She knew how Jill felt because she had felt the same about giving up Faith and Hope at first. At the time, she couldn't have been able to imagine not seeing them again. "It's not as hard as it seems, seeing your old horse," Josie said. "I mean, I was sad at first, but you do get used to it."

"Oh, I'm sorry," said Jill, reaching over to squeeze Josie's hand. "You know exactly how I feel. I'm sorry to bring it up."

"No, it's fine," Josie said.

"Well . . ." Jill hesitated. "If I did go back, what would Marmalade think? Suppose he's mad at me."

"Of course he wouldn't be mad at you," Josie said. "I'm sure he's really happy there. He'd probably be excited to see you!"

Still Jill looked unsure.

"And, once you're riding again you might even be able to take part in this fair that Josie was talking about," Mrs. Atterbury said.

"Do you think so?" said Jill, her face brightening. "It would be nice to get involved in some horse events again." She looked thoughtful. "But do you really think that Marmalade will be okay?" she asked Josie.

"Of course he will," Josie said. "You'd have the best of both worlds—both Marmalade and Faith around you. I can't imagine anything better."

"Well," Jill looked from Josie to her mom and back again. "Maybe it would be all right . . . if you come with me. Would you?"

"Definitely," said Josie.

"Okay then," Jill decided. "I'll go."

"Great." Mrs. Atterbury beamed. "I'll call Sally and set up a sidesaddle lesson for you."

She disappeared out of the room before Jill could change her mind.

"You really think it'll be all right, don't you, Josie?" asked Jill.

"Of course I do," said Josie. "And besides, it'll all be worth it if you can ride again."

Jill looked out of the window across the lawn and Josie could tell from the expression on her face that she was still worrying. But by the time her mother returned to the room, she seemed to be getting used to the idea.

"Well, that was easy enough," Mrs. Atterbury said, smiling. "Sally loves teaching sidesaddle and it's all been arranged. We can go and take a look around tomorrow," she said. "And if you approve, we can drop Faith off the day after that!"

CHAPTER FOUR

"Print," Josie murmured as she moved the mouse and clicked the icon on the screen in front of her. The printer whirred into action. Josie clicked on another arrow. The picture changed and someone riding sidesaddle flashed up. There were whole Web sites dedicated to the sport, pages full of clubs and competitions, even a group that met weekly to practice in Victorian riding clothes.

"'How to get the most out of riding sidesaddle,'" Josie read. She got up from her chair and gathered up the pages that had collected under her desk where the printer was. Sitting back on her heels, she flicked through the pile. "Jill will be really happy with all this," she said to herself.

"Josie, where are you?" Her mother's voice came from downstairs.

"Up here," Josie called back.

"Phone," yelled her mother.

Josie thought it was probably Jill, explaining why she was late. The Atterburys had arranged to pick up Josie at ten o'clock to go to Lonsdale and it was now ten past.

Josie grabbed the phone. "Jill?" she spoke into the receiver.

"Uh . . . no. Hi, Josie, it's Anna . . ."

"Oh, hey, Anna," Josie said. "Sorry. I thought you were going to be Jill. She was supposed to pick me up at ten. How are you?"

"Fine," said Anna. "I was just wondering if you'd like to come to Lonsdale with me today, but if you're already busy . . ."

"Lonsdale?" Josie asked. "I'm actually going there today, so I can meet you."

"Oh?" Anna asked.

"With Jill," Josie explained. "She's taking a look at the barn to see if she wants to keep Faith there so she can learn to ride again. She's going to try sidesaddle to help her hip. Isn't that great?" Josie exclaimed. When Anna did not respond, Josie sat down. "You're very quiet," Josie said. "Is something wrong?"

"No, nothing's wrong," said Anna. "I'll just meet you at Lonsdale, okay? Bye."

"Sure," Josie said, feeling puzzled as she put down the phone. Anna had sounded really strange.

When Josie turned to walk back up the stairs, she saw a big blue car pull up outside the gate to the house. She waved out the window as Jill got out. "I'll be right there," Josie called. "Mom, Dad, Jill's here. I'll see you later." She ran down the stairs, grabbing her sweater from the armchair in the hall.

"Bye, Josie," Mrs. Grace called from the kitchen. "Have fun."

Josie closed the front door behind her and got into the car. "Hi," she said, sitting down next to Jill. "Look what I've got for you," she said to her friend, spreading the pictures out over Jill's lap as Mrs. Atterbury drove down the road.

"They're great!" Jill laughed. "Look at this," she said, pointing to a rider in a full black riding habit. "I hope Lonsdale won't make me get dressed up like that every day. So what do you think the place will be like?" she asked. "Have you ever been there?"

"No, I haven't," said Josie. "But I'm sure it will be great. That's what Anna says—she's going to be down there today. She and her brother, Ben, are my friends." Josie was pleased to see Jill smile. Soon they were driving through a little town and then they were out in open countryside.

"It's not far," said Mrs. Atterbury, turning down a side road. They began to drive up a long bumpy road with fields and paddocks on either side.

"There it is." Josie pointed ahead to where a sign for Lonsdale directed them to the right. She wound down her window and looked out. The fields were enclosed by wooden fencing, and horses and ponies grazed peacefully, swishing their tails at the midday flies.

As they turned down the road they saw a big outdoor ring where a lesson was going on. Horses and riders trotted around the ring and, in the center, an instructor in jodhpurs was calling out instructions.

"Sit deep in the saddle, Isobel . . . that's it, Freddie, don't forget to change your diagonal as you cross the ring."

Mrs. Atterbury pulled up to a halt. "Should I drop you here?" she suggested. "Then you can watch the lesson and walk around. I'll come and get you in a couple of hours."

"That would be great. Thanks, Mom," said Jill as they scrambled out of the car.

"Come on, let's explore," said Josie.

Mrs. Atterbury drove back down the road and Josie and Jill watched a lesson for a few moments. Then they made their way on up the road, stopping by one of the pastures.

"Look at him. Isn't he gorgeous?" Josie said, pointing to a bay that was cantering across the field.

"And these are pretty cute too," said Jill, leaning over the fence to scratch the noses of a couple of Shetlands. She reached deep into her pocket and found a couple of mints. The Shetlands lipped up the offerings, crunching happily.

"Let's go to the barn," Josie said finally.

The drive parted into two and the barn stretched out ahead of them at the top of the road. A square of green grass was surrounded on four sides by whitewashed loose boxes. All around the barn, horses' heads looked out over Dutch doors as riders and grooms hurried around. There were hanging baskets filled with pink geraniums between the stable doors. Everything looked clean and well ordered and Josie started to have a really good feeling about the place.

A woman with a friendly face walked over to greet them. "Hello, I'm Sally. Can I help you?"

"I'm Jill Atterbury," replied Jill.

"Oh, yes, your mom called yesterday. You used to own Marmalade, didn't you? Your mom said you might like to bring your new horse, Faith, here to learn to ride sidesaddle."

Jill nodded. "And this is my friend, Josie. She used to be Faith's owner," she explained.

Sally nodded. "Pleased to meet you, Josie," she said. "Why don't I start by showing you where everything is? Then you can look around for yourselves. The buildings up there are the feed rooms and the hay barn. And to the left we've got more storage and here's the tack room." She showed them into a room at the right of the yard. "Well, I say tack room, but it's more than that. This is where everything happens."

Josie and Jill stepped into the cozy little room.

Along the back wall there were racks upon racks of saddles and bridles. Comfy old armchairs were scattered around. The room was cluttered and untidy, but it had a horse smell that made Josie feel instantly at home. Josie saw a glossy book on the desk.

"It's help for the fair we're putting on in a couple of weeks," Sally told her, noticing Josie's gaze. She picked up the book and showed them a picture. Knights were jousting, people were playing musical instruments, and kings and queens sat at tables.

"Anna told me about this," said Josie. "It sounds like a lot of fun."

"Oh, you know Anna?" Sally asked. "She and Ben are such a big help here."

Josie grinned. "Anna's my best friend," she explained. "My mom's been talking to Anna's mother, Lynne, about taking part in the fair too. I've got my own horse, Charity, and Mom thought she would ride a friend's."

"Well, that would be great," said Sally, sounding pleased. "Lynne's been great about coordinating everyone for this event. She's even managed to get a commentator for the day, so I only need to get the horses together." She looked at her watch. "I should get going. Just make yourselves at home. Marmalade should be coming in from a hack soon if you want to say hello."

"Thanks." Jill nodded uncertainly and Josie could tell that her friend was still worried about seeing her old horse.

"Let's go and find Anna," said Josie, trying to take her mind off it.

As Josie and Jill stepped outside into the yard, Josie saw Anna disappear into a stall on the right. It was bright after the dark of the tack room and Josie had to shade her eyes. The lesson from the outdoor ring was over and riders clattered into the barnyard, dismounting and untacking their mounts. As they approached the stall, Josie and Jill could hear Anna singing inside. She was obviously hard at work.

Josie smiled as she heard her friend's voice echo around the box. "Practicing for a contest?" she teased, poking her head over the stall door to see Anna bending down beside a light bay gelding.

"Oh, Josie," said Anna. Her head popped up

from beside the horse's feet. "You made me jump," she said.

"Come on," Josie said, drawing back the bolt and stepping inside. "Aren't you going to introduce me to this sweet horse?"

"This is Skylark," Anna said a little grumpily.

"This is Jill," Josie said, introducing Jill who was standing behind her. "She's Faith's new owner."

"Yes, I know that," Anna replied. "Hi, Jill," she said, turning straight back to Skylark.

Josie felt embarrassed. This wasn't like Anna at all—she was normally so chatty and friendly.

"He's a beautiful horse," Jill said, reaching in to stroke him.

"Isn't he?" Anna seemed to brighten up. "I used to ride Hope a lot at School Farm, but Skylark is pretty sweet too," she added.

"He reminds me of Marmalade, in a way," said Jill. "Except Marmalade's twelve point two, a couple of hands smaller."

"Oh, right," said Anna. "You used to own him, didn't you?" She turned and looked interested. "Have you seen him?"

"No, not yet," Jill admitted.

"Let's go and find him," Josie said. "See you later, Anna. Do you want to come over after? We could take turns riding Charity."

"Thanks, but I'm already busy," Anna said quickly.

"Oh?" Josie said, looking surprised. "What are you up to?"

"Mel's invited me to her house tonight," Anna replied, avoiding Josie's gaze. "But maybe some other time."

"Okay." Josie shrugged, feeling hurt. "But we'll speak tomorrow, right?"

"Sure." Anna nodded.

They left Skylark's stall. Josie was puzzled. It wasn't like Anna to turn down an opportunity to ride. "Come on, Jill," she urged. "Let's go and find Marmalade. I bet you're dying to see him!"

But Jill had already stopped and was looking to the other side of the yard where a horse was being untacked. "There he is," she whispered. "That's Marmalade."

Josie looked over to where Jill was pointing. A little bay gelding stood, soaking up the sun, his ears twitching back and forth.

"Come on." Josie tugged at her arm.

But Jill refused to move. "I don't think I should," she said. "What if he's mad at me?"

Josie was about to drag Jill over, but then she saw the tears in her friend's eyes. Jill was serious about this, Josie realized.

"I want to go home," Jill said. But it was too late. The girl with Marmalade was already leading him across the paddock. The horse stopped still for a moment.

"Come on, Marmalade," the girl scolded. "Don't be stubborn."

But Marmalade still wouldn't move. Then, before the girl could do anything, he let out a loud whinny, dragged the reins out of her hands, and trotted across the yard to Jill and Josie.

"Marmalade!" the girl called, desperately trying to get him back.

The horse stopped in front of Josie and Jill, nudging Jill's hands and whinnying gently.

"Oh, Marmalade," Jill cried, the tears welling up in her eyes. "You silly boy!" She buried her head in his mane and wrapped her arms around his neck. Marmalade nuzzled her pockets. "And you haven't

forgotten where I used to keep your treats either."
She smiled and reached inside her jacket pocket to
pull out a handful of mints. The horse munched
contentedly, his eyes slowly closing as he rested his
head on Jill's arm.

"Jill used to own Marmalade," Josie explained to
the girl holding Marmalade's halter.

"Well, he obviously hasn't forgotten her." The
girl grinned. "I'm Katie, by the way," she added.

"And I'm Josie." Josie smiled.

After a few moments, Katie said, "I need to take
Marmalade off and give him a quick rubdown. He's
booked in for another ride in a couple of hours and
he'll need a rest before then," she said.

"Of course," Jill said. Then she turned to look at
Katie. "I don't suppose I could groom him for you,
could I? It's just that I haven't seen him for a while."

Katie hesitated. "Well, I don't know," she said.
"We're supposed to groom the horses ourselves after
we've ridden them."

"We used to do that at School Farm, too," Josie
said. "My parents' old riding stables," she explained.
"But it wouldn't do any harm just this once, would
it?" she asked persuasively.

Katie looked thoughtful. "I guess not," she said at last. "And it would give me a chance to refill some water buckets and get him his hay." She smiled. "Here you are," she said, handing the reins over to Jill. "His stall is over there," she pointed. "And there's a grooming kit inside."

"Thanks." Jill took the reins and led the horse off in the direction of his stall. Josie smiled as she watched them go. "I'll see you in a moment," she called after Jill.

"Sure," Jill answered, smiling.

Josie wandered off to the back of the yard deep in thought. She was glad to see Jill looking so happy, but a tiny doubt crossed her mind. Will Jill still make time for Faith now that she's found Marmalade again? Josie wondered.

She came to a gate that led out into the fields and a sudden thought took her mind off her troubles. "This must be where the fair will be!" she said to herself. As she stood there in the gentle breeze she could almost see the fair now. In her mind the green fields in front of her weren't empty, but filled with knights jousting, jesters dancing, and minstrels playing. The carnival colors swam before her eyes.

"Josie, there you are . . ."

The picture faded and the field was empty once more. Josie turned to see Sally behind her.

"How are you doing?" Sally asked.

"Great," Josie said. "Lonsdale is very nice."

"I'm glad you like it," Sally smiled. "You're welcome any time. So . . . you know Faith better than anyone else. Do you think she'll be happy here?"

"Definitely," Josie said.

"And Jill? Has she made any decisions yet?" Sally asked.

"I guess we'd better ask her that," Josie said. "She's grooming Marmalade."

Josie almost felt bad disturbing the pair when she looked in over the stall door. The bay horse was resting his head on Jill's shoulder, his ears twitching back and forth as she stroked him.

"He's got you just where he wants you," Sally commented.

"He's so wonderful," Jill said, looking completely at ease with her old horse. "He's obviously happy here, but I have missed him."

Sally nodded gently. "So?" she prompted. "What

do you think? Should we start preparing a stall here for Faith?"

"You bet," said Jill.

"Good." Sally looked pleased. "Now, I'll leave you to say your good-byes and we'll see you tomorrow. I look forward to meeting your horse."

Once Sally was gone, Josie turned to Jill. "Didn't I say that you'd like it here?"

"Oh, Josie," Jill grinned. "It's the best. I can't believe how silly I was. If it wasn't for you I'd never have even come and looked around. And now I get to see Marmalade again, and Faith and I are going to be able to learn to ride sidesaddle. I can't believe how it's all worked out."

"It's perfect," Josie said, laughing.

CHAPTER
FIVE

"You should have heard him whinny, Dad," said Jill as she and Josie sat down with Mr. Atterbury for breakfast the following morning. "He was really happy to see me."

Josie had got to Jill's house early so that she could be there when the trailer arrived to take Faith over to Lonsdale.

"All right, all right," Mr. Atterbury teased. "That's now the fifth time that I've heard the story."

"And Faith's going to have her own stall, and I'll be able to go and look after her whenever I want—just like I do now," Jill added.

"That's great," Mr. Atterbury smiled. "I'm just

going to help your mom outside. I'll see you in a minute!"

Josie had been quiet during this exchange, pushing her cereal around her bowl. There was something that had been bothering her since yesterday, but she didn't know how to say it.

"Are you all right, Josie?" asked Jill.

"Yes, I'm fine," Josie replied. "I was just thinking about Faith . . . and Marmalade."

"Oh, Josie," Jill said, suddenly reading Josie's thoughts. "You're not worried that I won't have enough time for Faith now that I've seen Marmalade again, are you?"

Josie felt relieved that Jill had voiced exactly what she was thinking and that she hadn't had to say it herself. "Well, it had crossed my mind," she admitted.

"Oh, Josie, how could you think that?" said Jill. "Marmalade will always have a special place in my heart—he was my first horse, and it was horrible having to give him up. But Faith's different. She's gentle and kind and she doesn't even mind that I can't ride her. With Marmalade—well, he's lively and mischievous. I couldn't cope with that sort of horse now."

Josie smiled as she stood up to take her plate over to the dishwasher. "I know you love Faith," she said. "I never really doubted that. But I was worried how you felt after seeing Marmalade again."

"Don't be silly." Jill pushed back her chair as a car horn sounded outside. "I want to spend as much time as I can with Marmalade, but that doesn't mean I'll neglect Faith."

Josie understood. After all, she had Charity, but she would never forget about Faith and Hope.

"Now, come on." Jill grinned. "That'll be the man to take Faith to Lonsdale. Let's go."

The two girls rushed out of the kitchen and into the yard. To the right of the field, a trailer stood waiting. Jill's parents were at its side, and a man was undoing the ramp.

"Hi, I'm Mr. Ramsay," he said, turning to smile at Jill. "And this little lady," he nodded in the direction of Faith, "is going to Lonsdale, I understand."

"She certainly is," said Jill. "I just have to catch her."

Josie and Jill stood at the side of the fence as Faith came trotting over. In a split second, Jill had slipped the halter on Faith's head and was leading her to the trailer. "It'll be strange not having her here," she said.

"But it's not going to be for long," Josie reminded her. "Just until you're riding again."

"That's true." Jill nodded.

Faith stood for a moment at the bottom of the ramp and then carefully made her way inside.

Then Mr. Ramsay closed the ramp behind her. "I'll meet you at Lonsdale," he said to Mrs. Atterbury as he walked to the cab of the truck attached to the trailer.

"And I'll see you later this evening," said Mr. Atterbury. "I've got to head off for work now."

"Bye, Dad." Jill waved to her father. When he was out of sight, she turned to Josie, grabbing her arm and pulling her over to the car. "Isn't it exciting?" she said as they climbed in.

Josie grinned back, feeling relieved that Jill didn't seem to mind too much that Faith was going to be living somewhere else for a while.

Soon Mrs. Atterbury was driving behind the trailer as it made its way down the country roads. Jill's sidesaddle was in the trunk and Faith's bridle lay across Jill's lap.

"What time's your first lesson?" Josie asked.

"Three o'clock," Jill said excitedly. "Sally told Mom she wanted to give Faith enough time to settle in and get used to her new surroundings."

Mrs. Atterbury turned the corner and drove up the drive to the stables. This time she headed right into the barnyard. The trailer was there already and Mr. Ramsay was unbolting the ramp. Sally stood by his side, giving instructions. Already there was a group of riders eagerly awaiting the new arrival.

Sally waved and came over as Josie, Jill, and Mrs. Atterbury got out of the car. "Did Faith load okay?" she asked, nodding in the direction of the trailer.

"Faith never has a problem with that," Josie assured her, smiling as they watched Mr. Ramsay go to get Faith.

Jill rushed forward as Faith appeared at the top of the ramp and looked inquisitively around the yard.

"She's a beauty," remarked Sally. "How old did you say she was?"

"Twenty-two," Josie said proudly.

"Well, you'd never know it," said Sally. "She doesn't look a day over twelve. She's obviously been well cared for."

Josie watched as Faith's nostrils twitched and she strode down the ramp, arriving in a trot at the bottom. Josie walked over to pat her neck and Jill took the halter, stopping to give Faith a quick rub between her eyes.

It wasn't just riders who had gathered to see the new arrival. Horses and ponies looked over their Dutch doors. It was a welcoming sight—grays, blacks, bays . . . and there was Marmalade, too. Josie smiled when she saw the bay horse lift his head over his stall to survey the scene.

Faith sniffed the air and snorted. Then she raised her head and let out a loud whinny, her eyes bright and alert.

"She said she's going to like it here." Josie laughed.

"Oh, Faith." Jill gave her horse a big hug. "I know it's not home, but I hope you're going to be very happy. It's just for a few weeks—while I learn how to ride again."

"I've prepared a loose stall for her over there," said Sally. "Why don't you take her on over while your mother and I fill out the paperwork?"

"Great." Jill nodded, leading Faith off.

"I think I'll just go and see Anna," said Josie, noticing her friend in the far corner of one of the stables. "I'll be back in a sec."

"Okay," said Jill.

"Hey, Anna," Josie called over to where her friend was sweeping up the aisle. "How was last night?"

"Last night?" Anna echoed, looking puzzled.

"You were going over to Mel's house," Josie reminded her.

"Oh that," said Anna. "I didn't go in the end. Mel was too busy—something else came up."

"Oh." Josie was surprised. "You should have given me a call. You could have come over and played around with Charity."

"Yes, well I had other things to do," Anna said, shrugging. "You know, life doesn't just revolve around you, Josie Grace."

"I know that," Josie said, feeling stung by Anna's words. "I just thought that if you were free you might have liked to do something."

Anna didn't reply. She had already turned back to her broom and was attacking the aisle with new energy.

"Hey, Anna." Josie grabbed her friend's arm. "Is there something wrong? What is it? You're being really strange with me. Are you cross that I'm here at Lonsdale?"

"Why do you always have to assume that everything revolves around you?" Anna said angrily. "You and Charity . . . you and Lonsdale . . . well, no, I'm not bothered about you being here. In fact, I couldn't care less about you being at the stables at all. . . ."

"Whoa, hold on," said Josie, holding her hands in the air. "Calm down. I never meant to upset you," she insisted, puzzled at her friend's outburst. "You're not exactly being fair. I mean, I did ask you over last night."

"Big deal," Anna muttered under her breath as she jabbed the broom into the corner.

"What's wrong, Anna?" Josie persisted.

But Anna was silent.

"Well, if you're not going to tell me what it is, then I really don't see what I can do," Josie said, starting to feel angry.

Anna turned to Josie, her face red. "Oh, just leave me alone," she said.

"Josie? Josie can you come here a minute?" Jill's voice called from behind.

"I'll be right there," Josie called over her shoulder. She turned back to Anna. "Anna, maybe you'll call me when you aren't being so mean," she said coolly. And before Anna had a chance to say anything, Josie turned and marched off across the yard.

Josie knew she shouldn't have said that. It was a low blow, but Anna had deserved it after all the things she'd said. *But she's your best friend*, a little niggling voice said in her head.

"What's wrong?" Josie asked, as she reached Faith's new stall and put her head over the door.

"Oh, it's okay, I've got it fixed now," said Jill. "I just couldn't reach to tie up the hay bag."

"Well, she certainly seems pretty settled," Josie observed. She smiled as she watched Faith munching on her hay.

"She is." Jill grinned. "And here's my mom now."

Josie turned and saw Mrs. Atterbury walking across the yard toward them, deep in conversation with Sally.

As the two women drew near, Mrs. Atterbury

turned to Jill. "Well, it's all sorted out," she said. "I'll pick you up at four."

"Okay," Jill said happily. "But can I show you Marmalade first? Come and say hello to him."

"All right," Mrs. Atterbury said.

"I'll come with you," Josie offered.

As they walked across the barn to the stable, Jill called out to him. "Marmalade!" But there was no sign of him. Jill and Josie looked in over the Dutch door. The bay horse was in the corner of his stall but he didn't even look around at their approach.

"Marmalade, you've got visitors," Sally said, pulling back the bolt and letting Jill step inside. But Marmalade still didn't move.

"Marmalade, it's me," Jill said desperately. "Aren't you pleased to see me today?"

"He's probably just hungry," said Mrs. Atterbury.

Josie wasn't so sure. She had seen this sort of behavior before, and if she wasn't mistaken, Marmalade was sulking.

"He really did seem happy to see me yesterday," Jill said, her eyes showing disappointment.

"I'm sure he was, darling," said her mother.

"Do you think he saw me with Faith and that's upset him?" asked Jill.

"I don't know," Josie said. "Maybe . . ."

"He's certainly acting as though he's a little jealous," said Sally.

"Oh, dear," said Jill. "Poor Marmalade. I can see how it looks. One day I come back to visit him, and then the next, I arrive with a new horse."

"I'm sure he'll be all right in a while," said Josie. "He can't sulk forever."

"Why don't you spend some time with him before your lesson?" Mrs. Atterbury suggested. "Show him that you still love him."

"That's a good idea." Jill brightened up at the suggestion. "I could groom him, maybe take him for a walk. Would that be all right, Sally?"

"Of course," Sally replied. "We don't need him for a couple of hours."

"Perfect," said Mrs. Atterbury. "I'll be back to pick you up later."

Jill and Josie walked over to where Mrs. Atterbury's car was parked and waved her off.

As Mrs. Atterbury drove away, Josie turned to her friend. "Come on, Jill," she said. "Let's go and spend some time with Marmalade." She was anxious to put her run-in with Anna out of her mind too.

The two girls crossed back to the stall. A boy stood at Marmalade's door, talking to the horse. He looked about nine years old, a year younger than Jill.

"Hi, there," said Jill.

"Hi," replied the boy. "I'm Sam. I was just checking on Marmalade. He's my favorite," he added happily.

"I'm just about to give him a little bath," said Jill. "Would you like to help?"

"Sure!" said Sam.

Jill walked into the stall and led Marmalade out. They tied him up outside in the sunshine, and Josie ran off to fill a bucket of water from the tap. The water splashed into the bucket, then she carried it back over to Jill and placed it beside Marmalade.

"I haven't seen you here before," said Sam. "Are you new?"

"I guess you could say that," said Jill, starting to brush Marmalade down. "My horse, Faith, was brought here today. I'm going to start riding her this afternoon."

"You mean you haven't ridden her yet?" Sam's eyes widened.

"Well, not exactly," said Jill. She looked embarrassed.

Josie didn't know what to say to rescue her from the awkward situation.

"Why not?" Sam asked as Jill started to sponge the little gelding down.

"Er, just because," Jill said. Marmalade's ears twitched back and forth.

Jill walked around to his side to collect the hoof-pick from the grooming kit. Josie noticed that she was limping, and she guessed Jill was still stiff from riding Faith the other day. Suddenly, Marmalade kicked out his leg and the bucket of water went flying.

Jill wasn't quick enough to get out of the way and the water soaked her. "Oh, Marmalade," she cried in despair as she brushed down her jodhpurs.

"Are you okay?" Josie asked.

"Yes, don't worry, they'll dry in the sun," Jill sighed.

"Well, I'll just get you another bucket of water," Josie said. "Then I ought to go back home and ride

Charity. There's a bus that leaves in ten minutes, but I'll make sure I'm back in time for your lesson."

Josie went to fill another water bucket. She was just back in time to hear the tail end of Sam and Jill's conversation.

"What's wrong with your leg?" Sam asked.

Josie was relieved to see that there was a smile on her friend's face.

"I had an accident last year," Jill explained. "I haven't been able to ride since then. Marmalade used to be my horse. But when I couldn't ride him any more, we had to sell him to Lonsdale. Now I have Faith," she said. "Faith doesn't need as much riding—just a little each day. My friend Josie has been doing that for me up to now, but I want to take over."

Josie noticed that Jill had deliberately not mentioned the sidesaddle and wondered if she was still worried about it.

"Do you know many people here?" Sam asked.

"Not really," said Jill.

"Me neither," said Sam. "But Marmalade seems a bit bothered to see me today."

"I think that Marmalade's just being a bit of a

grump today, Sam," Josie joined in. "He'll be back to normal by tomorrow."

"Do you think so?" the little boy asked hopefully.

"I know so," Jill agreed, smiling at Josie.

Josie smiled back. It was good to see Jill looking relaxed.

As Josie jogged down the drive to catch her bus, she thought about the morning. It was great to see Faith settled. It was clear the horse was going to fit in at Lonsdale, and Marmalade—well, he would be back to normal soon enough. If only things were better with Anna. It was really strange. She was being so odd. She barely wanted to talk to her. In fact, Josie thought to herself, she was behaving no better than Marmalade!

Marmalade! Josie stopped as a thought grew in her mind. Could Anna be jealous of Jill in the same way that Marmalade was jealous of Faith? Could she be sulking too? After all, Josie and Anna had always done everything together. It must be strange for Anna now that Josie was spending so much time with Jill. But Anna could be a part of things. She'd always loved Faith, so she'd probably like to watch Jill's lessons. That was it, Josie decided. She'd talk to

Anna later that afternoon and make her understand, then everything would be all right.

"Hurry, Josie Grace, hurry," Josie muttered under her breath as she ran up the drive and into the yard at Lonsdale. She looked at her watch. She was late. It was ten past three, and she'd promised to be there in time to watch Jill's first lesson. Out of breath, she turned the corner. . . .

"Josie! You're here!" Jill waved from where she was sitting on Faith in the middle of the yard. "We got delayed a bit, so you haven't missed anything," she added.

Josie felt a rush of relief to see Jill looking so calm and happy on the mare's broad comfortable back. Faith's dark bay coat shone in the bright sunshine and the stripe on her face and her four socks gleamed white. "Faith looks wonderful," she said.

"Are you ready?" came a voice from behind her. It was Sally, coming out of the tack room.

"You bet," said Jill as Sally handed her a crop.

"Just sit very still," Sally told her. "Don't worry about giving aids just yet. Faith will follow Josie to the outdoor ring."

"How does it feel?" Josie asked as they walked slowly out of the yard.

"A bit odd at the moment—as if I'm going to fall off the right side," Jill confessed.

"You'll be fine in a minute," said Josie. "How was Marmalade today?"

"If anything, he was worse," said Jill. "I tried everything. I took him out for a nice long walk, I stroked him—but nothing. But I don't want Marmalade to spoil my sidesaddle lesson," she said as Sally opened the gate to the outdoor ring.

"I'm going to start you on the lunge," said Sally.

As Josie jumped up onto the railings to watch, she saw Jill's face fall.

"Just for the first couple of lessons," Sally said firmly. "I need to get Faith to start leading on the right leg so that your weight is properly balanced, otherwise you'll compensate by leaning out to the left." She went over to the bay mare and attached the lunge line. Then she walked out into the middle of the ring, letting it out. Finally, she clicked Faith on into a walk. "Try not to lean forward," Sally advised. "Keep the reins nice and long. Right shoulder back. That's it."

After a few minutes Sally turned to where Josie was sitting. "She's looking good, isn't she?" she called. Then she turned back to Jill. "Try to keep the weight on your right side."

Jill nodded, frowning with concentration. But she looked much more comfortable, and Josie was relieved. After thirty minutes of schooling, they slowed to a halt.

"You're a natural, Jill," Sally called. "You've made a pretty good start, so I think you should call it a day for now."

"Already?" Jill looked disappointed. "I was really enjoying that."

"I know," Sally said, smiling. "But it's important to end on a high note. Besides, your hip might be sore, and I think you'll find yourself a little stiff tomorrow morning—you use very different muscles riding sidesaddle," she continued, following the girls as they walked up the driveway.

As they reached the barnyard, it was buzzing with activity. "The afternoon hack is back," Sally explained, waiting for Jill to dismount.

"How did it go?" asked Sam, running over.

"It was great," Jill said as he stood by Faith's side.

"Now, this is the tricky bit—getting down," she said as she swung her right leg over the top pommel. Then, resting her weight on the pommel, she twisted and slipped neatly to the ground. "There," she puffed. "It's a lot further down from a sidesaddle than a normal one. Oh, Faith, you were terrific," she said, petting her horse's neck.

Faith nickered and Josie smiled. "I think she's trying to say you were terrific too," she said. "Here, I'll help you cool her down."

"Wasn't Faith great?" Jill said to Josie as they led the bay mare back to her stall. It was very busy, and Jill had to wade through a sea of riders. Marmalade was standing with a rider at the other end. Josie put a hand on her friend's shoulder.

"It's all right, Josie," said Jill. "Marmalade has to get used to seeing me with another horse."

As she walked away, Josie heard Marmalade let out a high-pitched whinny that had everyone's heads whipping around.

Jill went bright red. "It's all right," she soothed Faith, whose head had shot up in alarm. "Everything's okay."

Josie stopped to watch. As Jill led Faith past

Marmalade, he let out another loud whinny and shook his head.

What happened next, happened so quickly that even Josie didn't see it coming. Marmalade threw his head up, the force of the movement snapping his reins. Quick as a flash, he wheeled around, lashing out with his heels. The full force of the kick hit Faith squarely on the fetlock.

"Faith!" Josie cried, sprinting across the gravel to the horse's side.

CHAPTER SIX

As Josie got closer, she saw Jill holding Faith's head and trying to comfort her. Josie could see Faith's leg was already beginning to swell.

In an instant, Sally appeared at their side, calling out instructions. "Katie, call the vet! Get him to come immediately."

Katie nodded. "Okay," she said, dashing off.

Marmalade had been caught and now stood on the other side of the yard. But Josie didn't even want to think about him now. All she could think about was her Faith, standing beside her in pain. Josie forced herself to look at the blood trickling slowly from the wound and felt sick.

"Don't worry, Faith," Jill soothed, the tears streaming down her face. "The vet will be here soon. How could I have been so stupid?" she wailed to Josie. "I should have known something like this would happen."

"Don't be silly. You couldn't have seen this coming," Josie said, feeling helpless.

"It's all my fault," Jill insisted. "I shouldn't have let Faith walk so close to Marmalade."

"It's okay, Jill," said Sally. "The vet will be here soon. We should try and get Faith into her stall."

Josie followed as Jill led Faith, hobbling on three legs, to her stall. Josie tried to be brave for her friend, but it was just as bad for her, seeing Faith in pain.

"Try to make Faith as comfortable as possible," Sally said gently. "I'm going to get our first-aid kit."

Jill led Faith into the stall and gently stroked her nose. "Keep talking to her, Josie," she said. "It seems to comfort her." She went on rubbing circles on Faith's nose. Faith closed her eyes.

"Oh, Faith," Josie whispered, the tears welling up in her eyes. "You're going to be all right. You will, I promise."

At that moment, there was the sound of footsteps and Josie looked up to see Anna standing in the doorway.

"Josie, what's going on? Is Faith all right?" she asked. "I was in the outdoor ring, but Katie came to tell me what had happened." All traces of their earlier argument seemed forgotten.

"We don't know exactly," Josie said, relieved that Anna still cared. "It all happened so quickly, but the vet's on his way."

"Poor thing," Anna murmured. "Mom's picking me up in a moment," she said. "But I'm going to tell her I want to stay with you and Faith."

"You should go," Josie said. "There's really nothing you can do here. I'll call you tonight and let you know how she is."

Anna looked doubtful.

"It's better that way," Josie told her. "Faith needs as little fuss as possible right now."

"Okay, but promise you'll call?" Anna said.

"I promise," Josie said. She sighed. The day that had started so well had ended in disaster. Was it really only that morning that a happy, healthy Faith had been brought to Lonsdale?

At that moment, she heard more people approaching, and a man she hadn't seen before looked into the stall.

"Hello, I'm Dr. Dawson, the vet," he said. "Mind if I come in and take a look." He carried a bag into the stall. "What's her name?"

"Faith," said Jill.

"Hello there, Faith," he said.

Josie and Jill stepped outside and waited.

"If only I hadn't come to Lonsdale," Jill berated herself. "I knew it was a mistake. . . ."

"You couldn't have known this would happen," Josie soothed her.

Sally and Dr. Dawson were talking quietly as Jill paced up and down on the gravel. It seemed like ages before the vet came out and walked over to them.

"It's a bad bruise," he said gently. "The wound will need to be looked after properly."

"But it will heal, won't it?" Jill interrupted.

"It should, but you'll need to keep it as clean and dry as possible," Dr. Dawson told her. "And she mustn't be ridden for a couple of weeks."

"I don't care about that." Jill responded. "I just want her to get better."

"I've bandaged it up for the moment and she'll need a course of antibiotics so that she doesn't get an infection in the wound," the vet continued. "I'll come back in a couple of days to see how she's doing. The lady's taken quite a knock."

"Thank you for coming so quickly," said Sally.

"Yes, thanks, Dr. Dawson," said Josie and Jill.

The vet nodded and got into his car. Josie looked over the Dutch door into the stall. Faith stood in the corner, her head low, her eyes dull and listless.

"Are you all right?" Sally asked gently as she came back over to join them. "Faith will have to stay at Lonsdale to get better, and you heard what Dr. Dawson said—you won't be able to ride her for some time."

Josie felt really bad. Jill had been waiting for over a year for her specialist to say she could ride again. Now it looked like it would take even longer to ride again.

"You could always learn to ride on another horse," Sally suggested. "It wouldn't be impossible to find another suitable for riding sidesaddle."

"I don't know about that," said Jill. "It seems unfair to Faith somehow."

Josie looked at her friend. She could see that she was itching to continue with her lessons, but she was obviously worried about her horse. "You should keep riding," Josie told her. "You were doing so well, and plus, you'd be getting ready for when Faith is better."

"But I'm not really sure that I'd feel comfortable getting on a horse I didn't really know," said Jill.

"I can understand that," said Sally, looking sympathetic. "But what about Marmalade? You know him. . . ."

"But Marmalade is the one who kicked Faith!" Josie blurted out.

"It wasn't his fault," Jill said quickly. "He's a good horse. But even if I did want to ride him, the saddle wouldn't fit. He's much smaller than Faith."

"That's true." Sally looked thoughtful. "I'm afraid I don't have a sidesaddle I can offer you. There aren't that many people who want to learn these days."

Josie felt Jill's disappointment, and couldn't help feeling a bit guilty too. After all, it had been her idea for Faith to come to Lonsdale in the first place. If she hadn't suggested it, Marmalade would never have gotten jealous, Faith would be fine and Jill would still be learning to ride.

Suddenly, Josie had an idea. "Couldn't Jill ride another horse the same size as Faith?" she asked Sally.

"But I told you—I don't want to ride a horse I don't know," Jill started to say.

"But what if you did know that horse?" Josie asked excitedly. "Then how would you feel?"

"But there isn't another horse I know well enough," said Jill, running a hand through her hair.

"Yes, there is," Josie exclaimed. "There's Charity. She's built like Faith, and you know her well!"

For a moment Jill's eyes lit up, but then her shoulders sagged. "Oh, Josie, I'd love to ride Charity, but I couldn't do that to you," she said. "She's your horse. What would you do for the summer? She would have to come to Lonsdale to be stabled for at least two weeks. I bet you haven't thought about that!"

Josie stopped. Of course she hadn't. And she couldn't bear the thought of the gray mare living somewhere else. But this was Jill she was talking about—and Jill needed Charity more than Josie did right now. "But I'd be able to see her every day," she said. "And ride her occasionally," she added, glancing at Sally.

"Of course," said Sally. "And if it's any help, I'd be happy to stable her for free."

"It just seems like a lot to ask from everyone," said Jill.

"Well, if that's all that's stopping you, then I don't see what the problem is," Josie smiled.

"Well, maybe." Jill hesitated. "On one condition," she said. "That you ride with me. I know you won't be able to ride sidesaddle, but it would be fun to have some company in the lessons." She turned to Sally. "Would you be able to lend Josie a horse?"

"Of course I would," said Sally. "And it will be easier if there are two of you. You won't have to kick so hard if Charity has another horse to follow, and you'll just have to imagine you're riding sidesaddle, Josie," she said, laughing.

"So what do you think?" asked Jill, turning to Josie.

"Well, I don't know," Josie said. She didn't really want to take any more lessons. But then she saw Jill's eager face. Perhaps she should ride with her. Apart from everything else, it would be interesting to see how Charity did with a sidesaddle. "You're on," she said.

Slowly, Josie opened the door to her house and stepped inside. It had been a long day at Lonsdale, but finally Mrs. Atterbury had dropped her home. Now came the worst part—telling her parents what had happened to Faith. Her mother would be upset. The bay mare had been the first horse she'd bought for her riding school. Slowly, Josie made her way into the lounge where her parents were sitting. Josie's dad was watching the TV and her mother was reading the paper.

Her mother looked up. "Are you all right, honey?" she asked.

"Not really," Josie said and, seeing her parents' concerned faces, she crumpled. She'd been holding it in all day, putting on a brave face for Jill's sake, but now she let it all spill out—all about Marmalade, Faith's accident, the vet's diagnosis, and finally how she had decided to lend Charity to Jill. Her parents listened in silence until Josie looked up from where she had buried her head in her hands to see her mother's white face.

"You mustn't blame yourself, Josie," said her mom. "And it was kind of you to lend Charity to Jill. She'll make a good sidesaddle horse. Now, can you tell me exactly what the vet said again?"

"That she needs to rest for two weeks, that the cut needs to be kept clean and dry, and she has to be given antibiotics," Josie recited.

"Well, she's in the best possible hands," Mrs. Grace remarked. "So try not to worry."

It wasn't until Josie was in the bath that evening and the phone started ringing that she suddenly remembered—Anna! She'd promised to call her and tell her about Faith, but she'd completely forgotten to do it. Downstairs she heard her mother explaining what had happened. The words came up to her in fragments.

"Two weeks . . . yes . . . antibiotics." Her mother's voice drifted up to her.

Feeling guilty, Josie slid down in the bath again, letting the warm water seep over her. When she came up for air, she could hear her mother calling up the stairs. "That was Anna," she said. "I gave her an update on Faith and said you'd see her tomorrow."

"Thanks, Mom," Josie called back. For the first time she could remember, she was actually relieved that she hadn't spoken to Anna that evening. She didn't really feel like talking to anyone. She let out a big sigh. Poor Faith. So much had happened to her recently, between a new home and a new owner. And now she was in a strange stable and in pain. Josie felt as if she had been kicked as well.

CHAPTER
SEVEN

"Charity, we're almost there," Josie said, reaching down to pat her horse's neck as they strolled up the road to Lonsdale. When Josie had woken that morning she had almost forgotten what had happened the day before—and then it had all come flooding back and she had felt a little sad.

Josie clicked Charity into a trot. She could see Ben ahead of her in the yard. He was with a strawberry roan horse and seemed to be having trouble getting it to stand still.

"Hi, Ben," Josie said. "Have you seen Faith this morning?" She jumped down from Charity's back and lifted the reins over her head to tie her to a ring in the wall.

"Yes. She doesn't look very happy," said Ben, looking up from where he was picking out the horse's hooves. "Your mother's with her now. She dropped off Charity's grooming kit in the tack room for you." Ben turned back to Fleur's hoof and struggled a little bit to keep her still. "Could you hold Fleur's head for me?" he asked. "Every time I try to lift her foot, she whips her head around."

"Scared she might take a chunk out of your leg?" Josie said, trying to be lighthearted.

"Something like that," Ben said, laughing.

"I'll give Mom a few minutes alone with Faith, then I'll go over and say hello too," Josie said, holding Fleur still. "Hey, Ben. How is Anna today?"

"Fine." Ben looked puzzled. "Why?"

"Oh, nothing," Josie said. If Ben hadn't noticed anything, then Anna couldn't be too upset she'd forgotten to call last night.

Josie left Fleur and Ben and walked over to her mother. "How is she?" she asked.

"Poor thing," said Mrs. Grace, stroking Faith's nose. "I don't think she's touched her food today."

She nodded toward the hay in the corner of the stall.

Josie stroked Faith's nose. "Hi, Faith."

Josie could sense that Faith knew she was there and continued to pet her. But looking into Faith's eyes was too sad.

"I think I'll go and see what Sally has to say about Charity's stall," Josie said quickly. She didn't think she could keep the tears back if she stayed with Faith any longer.

"That's a good idea," Mrs. Grace said, nodding. "I probably won't be here when you come back out, I have to get home."

Josie understood. "I'll see you at home," she said. Walking across the yard, out of the corner of her eye, Josie saw Anna leading a big bay gelding into his stall. She followed her. In spite of Ben saying that Anna was fine that morning, Josie still felt guilty about forgetting to call.

"Hi, Anna," Josie said, leaning over the Dutch door.

"Oh, hi, Josie," Anna replied coolly.

"I just wanted to let you know that Faith's looking a little better today," said Josie.

"I know," Anna said abruptly. "I've already checked on her."

"Um . . . I wanted to talk to you about that," Josie began hesitantly. "I'm sorry I forgot to call you last night."

Anna still looked mad.

"I'm trying to apologize," Josie continued. "Can't we just be friends again?"

Anna was silent. But Josie could see from the look on her face that she was thinking. "I'm really sorry about the phone call." Josie looked at the ground and then back at her friend. There was still no response from Anna. "I have to go find Sally now, but could we do something together later?"

"Are you sure you've got the time to fit me in?" Anna snapped.

Josie had to bite her tongue to stop from snapping in return. Anna was still mad, and Josie didn't really blame her. She should have called her the night before. "I'll catch up with you later," Josie said. Frustrated, she turned and made her way to the tack room.

Sally was there, writing in the appointment book, her tortoiseshell glasses perched at the end of her nose. "Hi, Josie," she said. "I've just been moving around the rides for the day, trying to work out who's riding who. There's a hack going out at the same time as Jill's lesson, so most of the horses have been booked. I hope you don't mind—I've had to put you on Marmalade."

Despite what Jill had said about how sweet her horse could be, Josie was unsure of him because of what he'd done to Faith. Her feelings must have been easy to read.

"I know you're upset with Marmalade after what happened with Faith," Sally said gently. "But I think you should give him a chance. Besides, it would be good for him to see Jill riding another horse."

"But what if the same thing happens with Charity?" Josie said. "What if Marmalade lashes out at her?"

"I'll be keeping a close eye on everything in the lesson," Sally told her. "So I can promise you that won't happen."

Josie relented. She couldn't stay mad at any horse for long. "That's fine," she said. "Where should I put Charity?"

"The fourth stall on the right," said Sally. "Next door to Skylark."

Josie went outside to get her horse. Charity let out a little sigh when she saw her. "Yes, I know, you want to be out in the field." Josie grinned as she undid the girth and slid her own saddle down from Charity's back. "But you've got a bit more riding to do first."

"Hi, Josie," Jill called from her mother's car. "I'll give you a hand with that," she said, hurrying across the yard.

"Oh, hi, Jill," said Josie. "How are you feeling today?"

"A bit stiff after the sidesaddle work yesterday, but my hip's fine." Jill patted her hip and smiled. "Have you seen Faith yet?" she asked anxiously.

"Yes, and my mom came to check on her too," Josie said. "She's looking better than yesterday."

"That's good," said Jill. "I'm going to go see her and then come back in a few minutes."

Josie wanted to go with Jill, but Faith was her friend's horse now and she knew she should let Jill have some time alone with her.

After Josie settled Charity in her new stall and fed her, Jill came back. "Poor Faith, she's still looking pretty miserable. I'm so sorry, Josie."

Josie walked over to her friend and put her hand on her shoulder. "It's not your fault, Jill."

"It just feels like that," Jill said. "And I just heard that you're riding Marmalade."

"Yes," Josie said. She looked at Jill and decided to be honest. "Although I haven't completely forgiven him for what he did to Faith yesterday."

"Me neither," said Jill. "But let's give him another chance," she pleaded.

"I will," Josie said. "Let's go get tacked up."

Ten minutes later, Josie and Jill led their horses into the ring. It looked strange seeing Charity in a sidesaddle. Jill looked quietly confident after her lesson yesterday and, in spite of everything that had happened, Josie felt positive. Jill was riding again.

Charity gave Josie a puzzled look as Sally gave Jill a leg up in the saddle, but she stood quietly enough while Jill arranged her legs on the pommels.

"Have a great lesson, Jill," Sam called across from the edge of the ring.

"Thanks," Jill smiled back happily.

"Are we all ready?" asked Sally. She gathered Charity's lead rope in her hand.

"Definitely," Josie answered, making an effort to keep her distance from Jill and Charity. Marmalade was on his best behavior. He had a nice long stride even though he was smaller than Charity. Josie began to relax into the saddle as they rode around the ring.

"Remember everything I told you yesterday, Jill," said Sally. "Right shoulder back, left shoulder forward."

Jill was riding off the lunge today and seemed at ease as she walked Charity around the ring.

"Cross the ring at F, Josie," called Sally. "Change rein on the diagonal, that's good."

Josie felt a pang as they circled the ring. It had been a long time since she'd had a lesson—since her mother had been teaching at School Farm. There she would help her mother with lessons all the time. Marmalade might not be Charity, but he had a good stride and was well schooled. Josie glanced across the ring and was happy to see Anna watching from the fence. She knew that her best friend wouldn't stay mad at her long.

"Keep your hands up, Jill," Sally called. "You don't want to slip forward."

Jill nodded and corrected herself immediately. She was a quick learner, Josie realized. After another fifteen minutes, Sally announced, "I think you could try a canter today."

"Really?" Jill looked doubtful. "I tried a trot when I was at home and that was hard enough."

"A canter on a sidesaddle is much easier," Sally assured her. "When you're ready."

Jill pushed with her seat and gave Charity a little nudge with her crop. Charity picked up a canter around the ring, her stride graceful and relaxed. Josie and Marmalade stood at the side. Josie felt a surge of pride in her gentle horse. She leaned down to pat Marmalade's neck in case he felt left out. Marmalade was doing his part, too.

One more circle, and Jill drew Charity back down to a walk. "That was great," she said, her eyes lighting up.

"Okay," said Sally. "Another fifteen minutes and I think we'll call it a day. You've both worked pretty hard. I don't want to push you and then have a setback. We'll tackle a trot soon."

Jill groaned. "That's what nearly put me off sidesaddle forever!"

"I can imagine," said Sally. "It's the hardest part of sidesaddle. But once you've got used to that, you can do anything—even go out on a hack. Surely that's worth working toward?"

"That would be great," said Jill. "Wouldn't it, Josie?"

"Yes!" Josie said. It had been fun riding in the outdoor ring, but she preferred hacks any day.

All too soon their lesson ended. Josie looked for Anna, but she had already disappeared. As they rode back into the barnyard, the riders from the morning hack began coming in through the back gate.

Josie jumped down from Marmalade and led him over to the right-hand side of the barnyard. The gelding had been on his best behavior in the outdoor ring. It was like he was a different horse from the one they'd seen yesterday. It was as though Marmalade didn't seem to mind Jill riding another horse, as long as he had enough attention from someone else.

Josie noticed voices coming from near Charity's stall. Josie turned around, her eyes narrowing as she looked across the yard. Jill was there, with Sam and a group of girls. What was going on? Josie wondered. She walked closer, just in time to catch the tail end of the conversation.

"What's your problem, peg leg?" the tallest of the three girls said to Jill. Jill stood in the doorway, the weight of the sidesaddle on her arm. "Can't you carry your own saddle?" the girl said.

Jill's face was red. "It's heavier than a normal saddle," she said. "And I haven't got a peg leg, I just hurt my hip a long time ago."

"Can't you ride in a *normal* saddle then?" another girl sneered.

Josie felt her blood boil. She was just about to march over and say something when Anna appeared from Skylark's stable and stood, hands on hips, in front of the girls.

"Leave her alone, Amelia," Josie heard Anna say. "She's a better rider than you'll ever be—sidesaddle or not."

"Oh yeah?" said Amelia. "And what would you know about that, Anna Marshall?"

But Josie could see that the bully had been thrown off by someone standing up to her.

"I know because I saw Jill ride today—she did great, and it's only her second sidesaddle lesson!" Anna stood firm, raising her eyebrows as if to challenge Amelia.

For a moment, it looked as though Amelia was going to say something back, but then she seemed to think better of it. She turned on her heel and walked off, her friends trailing after her like sheep.

"What was all that about?" Josie rushed over.

"Oh, it's nothing," Jill said in a small voice. "I guess I brought it on myself really. They were teasing Sam about being small and I couldn't stop myself from butting in and sticking up for him."

"Thanks, Jill," Sam said. "They've been saying mean things for weeks, and Amelia's brother is in my class at school and he's just as mean as she is."

"I can imagine," said Jill. Then she turned to Anna. "And thanks, Anna," she added. "It's one thing sticking up for someone else, but I didn't know what to say when they started in on me."

"No problem," Anna shrugged.

"Well, we still have a couple of tired horses to take care of," said Jill. "Do you mind if I groom Marmalade and Charity?" she asked Josie. "I'd still like to spend a bit of time with him."

"Not at all," Josie said. "In fact, I wanted to check up on Faith. She needs grooming too. Want to come with me, Anna?" she asked tentatively.

"Sure," Anna said, following Josie off toward Faith's stall.

As they walked, Josie turned to Anna. "Thanks for sticking up for Jill," she said. "That was really nice of you. Those girls were really being mean."

"It was nothing," said Anna as she drew back the bolt to Faith's stall and stepped inside. "Anyway, I meant what I said. I did see Jill riding, and I really do think she's amazing."

Faith whickered when she saw them, and Josie felt her heart lift.

"I hate to see anyone bullied," Anna said. "Especially by that Amelia. She's such a snob. And she's not even a good rider!"

Josie smiled at her best friend as she started to run a brush over Faith's shoulders. "I really appreciate what you said." She hesitated. "Especially as I didn't think you liked Jill very much."

"That's not true, Josie!" Anna burst out. "I've got nothing against Jill. She's really nice. It's just—oh, I know I've been acting funny lately, but you seemed to be spending so much time with her. I guess I was worried you liked her more than me. I was just jealous, I guess," she finally admitted in a small voice.

Josie said, "You are my best friend, Anna."

Anna continued to brush Faith as Josie kept talking. "Anna," Josie said.

Anna looked up from stroking Faith's nose.

"Jill and Faith needed me," Josie said slowly. "And I didn't want to let them down. It doesn't mean I like you any less."

"I understand that now," said Anna. "Jill must think I'm a bad friend, the way I've been acting."

"She hasn't said anything to me," Josie promised. "And you are the best friend in the world." The girls hugged.

Anna smiled as Faith softly whinnied. The girls laughed. Faith seemed to be glad the fight was over, too. "My mom asked me if you wanted to come over for supper tonight. She's nearly finished all of the costumes for the fair and she thought you might like to have a sneak preview before she brings them to Lonsdale. I'm going to ask Jill over too," she said.

"You don't have to do that," Josie said gently.

"But I want to," Anna insisted.

Faith snorted from behind them, as if reminding them that she was there. "It's all right, Faith,

Anna and I are best friends forever," Josie said. "Right?"

"Right," Anna agreed.

"What do you think?" Lynne Marshall mumbled through a mouthful of pins. She stood up from where she'd been kneeling to put together the final costumes. "It's going to be for your dad, Josie."

Josie, Jill, and Anna looked up from the kitchen table at the jester's costume that Lynne held up. It was bright orange and red and had a little starred cap with bells on.

"It's terrific." Josie grinned. "Dad's going to look great in it!"

"I think so." Lynne Marshall grinned back, running a hand through her spiky blond hair. "Well, he said he wanted to help!"

"And what about this?" said Ben, holding up a gray costume.

"What is it?" Josie asked.

"Can't you tell?" said Ben. "It's a suit of armor. We couldn't get the real thing, so Mom made it. And this"—he held up a cardboard cone that had been sprayed silver—"is the helmet."

"It's great!" said Jill admiringly.

"And look at these," said Anna, lifting up two crowns also made of cardboard. "One for a king and one for a queen."

Josie smiled. She was so happy to think that Anna and Jill were now friends. "I wonder who'll get those parts," she said excitedly.

"Well, that's up to Sally," Lynne Marshall said. "I'm just in charge of the costumes. Sally will decide who's riding who and wearing what. It's going to be a fantastic event."

Josie grinned at Jill, Anna, and Ben. The medieval fair was going to be so much fun. But as Josie thought about the costumes she couldn't help but wonder. Would Jill be able to ride in the fair?

CHAPTER
EIGHT

"Up down, up down . . . try not to throw yourself out of the saddle, Jill," Sally called across the ring.

It was a week later, and Sally was teaching Jill how to trot while Josie watched from the railings. Jill and Charity had already been riding for a good half hour and clouds were gathering ominously overhead. It looked as though it was about to pour.

"You'll find that you won't want to do a posting trot much," Sally warned Jill from the center of the ring. "It can make your bottom ache."

She was starting Jill on the lunge again for this exercise. "Most sidesaddle riders sit to the trot, but I wanted you to see what it was like. How does it feel?"

"My bottom's fine, but my hip aches a little," Jill admitted as she pushed herself up. She had to use her seat to push up since she couldn't place too much pressure on the stirrup, because that would make the saddle lopsided.

"All right," said Sally. "I think you've done enough of that. You're ready for the sitting trot. You need to be supple and soft-backed when you sit in the saddle. Try to soften your back, but without slumping."

Jill nodded and Josie was pleased to see her friend relax. "Loosen your left leg, pull your knee down with your toe," Sally advised, holding out her hands as it started to sprinkle. "I think we'll have to wrap this up a bit sooner than I'd have liked," she said. "Still, you're making great progress."

Jill brought Charity to a halt. Josie walked forward to lead her out of the ring. Clapping her hand to Charity's neck, Jill looked very happy. "That felt great." She beamed.

"It looked great too." Josie grinned up at her. "What a difference from when you tried at home last week."

Jill nodded. As they walked into the barnyard, they saw a truck near the barn.

"That's Dr. Dawson's truck!" said Jill, putting Charity on a free set of crossties. "He must have come to see Faith."

They hurried inside the stable and looked into Faith's stall.

"How is she?" asked Jill.

"She's doing well," Dr. Dawson said, straightening up. "You've done a good job of looking after her. The cut is clean and healthy. I think we can probably take the bandage off." He ran his hand down her leg. "She's still got some bruising, but she's made good progress. I'll come back in a few more days to give you the verdict on when you can expect to ride her."

"Thanks for coming out, Dr. Dawson," said Jill. "Faith's very precious to me—well, to both of us," she added, looking at Josie.

"Yes," said Josie. "I've known Faith all my life. Thanks for checking up on her again."

"You're welcome," Dr. Dawson smiled. "I'm glad to see that she's doing so well."

Josie started to walk across the barnyard to untack Charity when she saw a familiar car coming up the drive—her parents'. The car pulled to a stop and Josie's mother stepped out.

"Hi, Mom," said Josie, surprised. "What are you doing here?"

"I have a meeting about the fair," her mother said.

"Oh," Josie said, nodding. With all the excitement of that morning, she had completely forgotten. They were supposed to be meeting in the tack room to discuss who was doing what. And just in time, Josie thought as she looked overhead. The sky was very dark, and it was raining more heavily now.

"You just missed the vet," Josie told her mother. "He said Faith's looking much better. She's still not ready to be ridden," she added, "but she's getting there."

"That's great news," said Mrs. Grace. "I'm going to say hi."

As Josie's mom walked into Faith's stall, Faith let out a loud whinny of delight.

"Hello, darling." Mrs. Grace stroked her old horse's neck.

Faith was shifting around in her excitement. "Hang on, calm down," Mrs. Grace soothed. "I don't want you to get overexcited. You need to rest that leg." Faith nuzzled at Josie's mom, nudging her hands for more attention.

"Come on, Mom," said Josie, looking at her watch. "We need to get to that meeting."

Josie could tell that her mother was reluctant to leave Faith, but finally she gave the bay mare one last pat and left the stall.

The rain was coming down now, so Josie and her mother had to make a dash across the yard. The tack room was already crowded when they arrived. There was just enough space to squeeze in.

Josie looked around the room at the friendly faces—Anna and Ben were there with their mom, and a man that Josie hadn't seen was standing behind them. Jill was sitting on the other side of the room with Katie and Sam . . . then there was Amelia Johnstone and her friends . . . and a few other faces that Josie recognized from around the stables. With the exception of Amelia, Josie felt a warm glow at the sight of all the new friends she had made. It wasn't the same as being at her own stables, but it was still a good place to be.

"Thank you all for coming today," said Sally, raising her voice above the din. Gradually, the noise subsided and everyone quieted down for the meeting to begin.

"As you all know, the fair is on Saturday—just a few days away. All of the costumes are finished thanks to Lynne Marshall, but there's a lot more to do."

Josie looked over and smiled at Anna. She knew her friend was very proud of her mom. The costumes were amazing.

"We need to work out who does what and then we need to make sure everyone knows their role in the fair," Sally continued. "It's the first time that we've done something like this, so there'll be lots of people coming to watch. The local paper's even going to come and take pictures. We want to make sure that we get it right, so there will be a 'dress rehearsal' on Friday afternoon."

There were little murmurs around the room

as everyone began to talk excitedly about the upcoming event. Josie, Jill, and Anna all showed big smiles.

"The fair will start at two," said Sally, glancing out of the window to where the rain was pelting down on the windowpanes. "Let's hope it's better than today! You should all be here by noon to get your horses ready and get what you need. As you know, the fair's based on a medieval tapestry." She held up the book, which revealed a brightly colored page. "Now, here's what I propose. We need a whole lot of characters—noblemen, knights, peasants, a king and queen, a falconer." She ran down the list. "And those are just the ones on horseback. Lynne's already got some people from town who are going to take part on foot as minstrels, jesters, and stilt walkers. Isn't that right, Lynne?"

Then Sally held up a picture of a medieval tapestry. Josie looked closely and saw the knights, peasants, a king, a queen, and even jesters and stilt walkers! Josie was getting really excited now.

"Sally," said a woman who Josie recognized

from Friendship House. "The children from Friendship House are coming with their horse, Hope."

Josie smiled at the thought of seeing Hope. She had known the gentle horse would be wonderful with the physically challenged children of Friendship House. Now those children could participate in the fair, too!

Sally looked down at a pad of paper. Josie was anxious to hear what her part would be in the fair. "Amelia, Isobel, and Mary," Sally began, "you will be noblemen, riding Lightning, Blackjack, Shadow, and Mary's bringing Connie with her."

Josie nudged her mother.

"Anna, Jack, Sam, and Ben . . . you're all going to be knights. I've got you down on Skylark, Puzzle, Minstrel—and Ben, you said you were bringing Tubber?"

"That's right," Ben replied. "A knight! Awesome!" he punched the air with his fist.

Sally raised her eyebrows. "Provided you behave like knights."

"Fat chance of that with Ben around," Anna grinned.

"And that, I think, just about covers everyone," said Sally.

"But, what about us?" Josie piped up. Sally hadn't mentioned her or Jill's name.

"How could I forget you two!" Sally smiled. "You and Jill are going to be heading up the parade as king and queen."

Josie couldn't believe her luck. It was the biggest honor of all!

"I had to think carefully about who could play those parts," Sally said with a twinkle in her eye. "The queen's costume is a beautiful long robe, so I needed someone with a special talent to be able to ride wearing it. Who better than Jill, who can ride sidesaddle? And Josie as the king can be her riding partner."

Josie grinned across the room at Jill. Even Amelia Johnstone couldn't ruin this one for them.

"Jill will be riding Charity, of course, and Josie will be on Marmalade," Sally finished.

With no encouragement from Sally, the room burst into a round of applause, led by Sam.

"Congratulations, Jill!" cheered a chorus of voices.

Jill blushed. Josie was proud of her friend's achievement. She'd worked so hard and done so much in the last week. There was just one thing missing. If only Faith could take part too, then everything would be perfect. But she'd heard what the vet had said that morning—her leg was healing well, but it was by no means perfect.

"Now," said Sally. She held her hand in the air to bring the cheering to a halt. "Let me introduce Jack Harvey." She indicated the man behind her. "He's going to be our commentator. I'll hand it over to him to explain a few things about how the fair is going to work."

"Hi there, everyone," said Jack, looking around the room. Jack was an older man with gray hair. He spoke in a gentle and calm voice as he explained how the fair would be run. Jack would stand at the podium and announce all the characters, giving background on the type of dress and their role in medieval times. Everyone would ride around the ring once.

Josie was going to burst with excitement! She turned again to her friends. They had the same look on their faces. The fair was going to be so amazing.

But then Josie thought of Faith. If Faith couldn't be in the fair, the day would not be perfect. And more than anything Josie wanted everything to be absolutely perfect.

CHAPTER
NINE

The next few days passed quickly as everyone prepared for the fair. Suddenly it was Friday morning, and Jill and Josie were having their last lesson before the dress rehearsal that afternoon.

"You and Charity are going to steal the show," Josie said, walking Marmalade out of the ring and into the driveway.

"Oh, Josie, don't be silly, I'm just wearing a green dress," Jill said, laughing.

"And riding sidesaddle!" Josie said. "Anyway, what are you looking so worried about?"

"Dr. Dawson's coming back today," Jill reminded her.

"I know," said Josie, a sudden pang of worry flooding through her.

Josie jumped down from Marmalade and led him off to his stall. As she started to untack him, she saw the vet's car drive up. She was itching to hear what he had to say about Faith, but Jill was already rushing over and Josie knew she should let her talk with the vet first. Josie turned back to Marmalade and started to run a brush over him.

"Are you done with your lesson on Marmalade?" Sam's voice called over the door. "Can I brush him?"

"Sure, if you'd like to," said Josie, holding the brush out and stepping back out of the stall. Marmalade gave a little whinny of recognition when Sam walked in.

"It's like he knows me now." Sam grinned as the horse nuzzled his hands affectionately.

Josie watched them over the stall door, her ears tuned in to what was happening on the other side of the barn where Sally and Jill were standing outside Faith's stall. Josie tried to concentrate on Marmalade. The horse looked relaxed and contented. Marmalade and Sam had been spending more and more time together and the bay horse certainly seemed to like having Sam around.

"Josie! Josie!" Jill's voice called, and suddenly she came running over in their direction. For a split second, Josie thought it was going to be bad news, but then she saw Jill's smiling face.

"Faith's leg's so much better," Jill beamed, her eyes sparkling. "All that patience has paid off. Dr. Dawson even said that she should have a little exercise today, so Sally suggested we take her out for a short walk."

"What's the news?" Anna called, rushing over and stopping in front of them.

"Faith's better!" Jill said.

"That's great!" said Anna, spinning Jill around in a big hug.

"I'm going to take her out in a minute," said Jill. "You should come too . . . Josie on Charity . . . and you on Skylark. Come on."

"Well, I don't know," Anna hesitated. "Sally hasn't said I can take Skylark out."

"Go on, Anna." Sally said from behind them. "You've all earned it. Plus, I could use a little quiet before the dress rehearsal."

"And you should go too, Sam," Sally said,

smiling at the curly-haired boy. "You can take Marmalade out. He's been the perfect gentleman this past week, so I'm sure that you won't have any trouble with him."

"Well, if you're sure," said Jill. "Then that would be perfect. All of my friends can be together—humans and horses!"

The afternoon sun was high in the sky as Josie and Jill mounted Charity and Faith. Ben had brought Tubber to Lonsdale in preparation for the dress rehearsal that afternoon. He tacked up the horse while Anna tacked up Skylark. As Sam led Marmalade out of his stable, there was a big grin on his face. Josie and Jill helped him with the tack. Then they all set off for the back gate to the fields and into the woods behind.

"Don't be out for too long," Sally warned them. "Remember the horses have already been ridden this morning, so they'll need to be watered and rested before the dress rehearsal."

"Of course," Josie said, bending down to stroke Charity's neck as the string of horses and riders filed through the gate and into the field. It was good to be back on her own horse. She had enjoyed riding

Marmalade, but nothing compared to Charity.

"Isn't this perfect?" Jill said looking around.

"It's the best!" Anna called back. "Want to trot?"

"What about Faith?" Josie said.

"Don't worry about me," said Jill. "Just wait for me on the other side of the field. I'll walk her over."

Josie took the lead and nudged Charity on. The horse responded with ease to her leg. As Josie felt the wind rush through her hair she couldn't resist pushing Charity into a canter. She looked around to check that Sam and Marmalade were behind her. Marmalade's ears were pricked forward, and the boy and horse looked perfectly confident.

As they drew to a halt, Sam's eyes were shining. "That was awesome," he said. "Marmalade's the best!"

Marmalade gave a whinny.

Josie smiled as she watched Jill and Faith meander over to them. Marmalade didn't seem remotely bothered about Jill riding Faith now. And he was clearly having a great time with Sam.

Once Jill had reached them, Josie followed her lead into a path in the trees, the shade from the branches providing welcome relief from the sun. As they wound their way through the trees, Josie couldn't think of anywhere else she'd rather be.

"We should head back to the stables," Jill said, looking at her watch.

As they followed the path back through the woods and into the fields, Josie rode up alongside Jill. In spite of how happy she had been earlier, Jill looked worried.

"I bet you can't wait to get Faith back home," Josie said.

"It's going to be great," Jill replied.

Josie was puzzled. Jill's words were enthusiastic, but she had said them very quietly. It was as though something was bothering her friend. "Is anything wrong, Jill?" she asked.

"It's just that—oh, you might as well know," Jill said. "It's about Faith. I've really loved riding Charity and all that. Don't get me wrong—she's been perfect through all of this. . . ."

"Yes?" Josie urged. She couldn't really see where this conversation was going.

"It's just that I can't help wishing I was riding Faith in the fair," Jill blurted out. "I hate the thought of leaving her out."

"Oh, Jill, why didn't you say something before?" Josie said as they reached the back gate. "I'm sure it could be arranged. You could ride Faith and I'd ride Charity instead. It would be perfect."

"I've thought about that," said Jill. "But where would that leave Marmalade? He'd be left out and we'd be back to square one. What if he starts to resent Faith again?"

It was true. Josie hadn't thought about that. The positions for the fair had been decided when they'd thought Faith couldn't be ridden. Now that the bay mare was fit again, things had changed. But all of the riders had been assigned horses, which would leave Marmalade riderless.

"You've got a point," Josie admitted. She couldn't see a way around it as she led Charity across the yard to her stall. And even if they could find another rider to take care of Marmalade, there wouldn't be a costume for the rider. "Maybe we could talk to Sally," she suggested, unbuckling Charity's bridle and saddle and slinging the bridle over her shoulder. "She might be able to suggest something."

"Oh no, don't do that," said Jill. "You saw how

stressed she was earlier. I don't want to bother her. She's been so great about everything."

"Well . . ." Josie hesitated.

"No, Josie," said Jill. "I know you want to help, but just forget that I said anything."

"I guess," Josie shrugged. But she still couldn't help feeling frustrated as she made her way to the tack room.

Sally and Lynne were there, poring over some paperwork for the fair. "So how was your ride?" asked Sally.

"It was good," Josie said, putting the saddle and bridle in their place and walking over to the table. Absentmindedly she picked up the glossy book with the medieval tapestry and glanced at the picture.

"Then why the gloomy face?" Lynne prompted.

"Oh, I don't know," said Josie. "The ride was perfect. It was so good to see Faith better and happy again. Jill rode her like a dream."

"I had a feeling that Faith would be the sort of horse who'd take well to being ridden sidesaddle," said Sally. "Jill must be very happy."

"Well," Josie hesitated. She had told Jill she would forget their talk about Faith and the fair. But

Josie had an idea. "Jill would really like to ride Faith in the fair."

Just then Josie heard footsteps behind her. Jill, Anna, Ben, and Sam clattered into the tack room to return their saddles. It felt a little like she was going behind Jill's back after she'd promised not to say anything.

Josie took a deep breath and continued. She picked up the picture of the medieval tapestry and pointed to a bay horse just like Marmalade with a page boy riding him. She looked at Sam. "Sam can ride Marmalade as a page boy, and then we'd be exactly like the picture!"

"What are you talking about?" Sally looked puzzled.

Jill looked at Josie, but Josie had to go on. She had to get Sally to agree to the plan.

"Look," said Josie.

Sally looked thoughtful. "Well, you're right. We certainly do seem to be missing a page boy."

Josie hesitated. She didn't want to look as though she was interfering. "Sam would be perfect for it," she explained.

"Yeah!" said Sam. "That would be cool!"

Sally sat silently and Josie held her breath as she looked at Sam's excited face.

"Well, it's certainly an idea," Sally said at last. "But we haven't got a costume."

"Maybe my mom could rustle up a costume," Anna said.

Josie smiled at her best friend.

"Oh, Anna." Lynne Marshall looked weary. "I don't know."

"But this is important, Mom, please," Anna pleaded.

"All right then," said Lynne. "I'll do it." She grinned.

"Thanks, Mom," Anna said excitedly.

"Would that really be all right?" Jill stammered. "I mean, I don't want to make any trouble."

"It's no trouble," Lynne promised.

Josie looked around at her friends' happy faces. Jill would be riding Faith, she would be riding Charity, Anna would be on Skylark, Ben on Tubber, and Sam on Marmalade. Now everyone had the perfect part in the fair.

CHAPTER TEN

Beep, beep, beep . . . The alarm clock went off and Josie opened one eye and stretched. She sprang out of bed and threw back the curtains. A stream of sunlight flooded the room. It was going to be a nice day for the fair! The rehearsal had gone well yesterday afternoon and everyone seemed ready. She scrambled into her riding clothes and ran down the stairs, carrying her costume under one arm.

"So, what do you think?" asked her father, holding up his jester's outfit.

"Oh, Dad, it's great." Josie laughed as her father danced around the kitchen.

"Just ignore him," her mother said, winking at

her. "Now, help me get ready," Mrs. Grace added as she looked at the suit that Lynne had put together for her. Made up of pants, a jacket, long silk stockings, and a hat with a quill in it, Josie's mom was going to look the perfect nobleman.

"You'll look fabulous, Mom." Josie gave her mother a quick hug. "Are we ready?"

The Graces piled into the car. The plan was for Josie's dad to drop off her mom at nearby stables to get Connie. Then she would ride Connie over to Lonsdale.

"Don't forget to take my costume in from the car," Mrs. Grace reminded them as she got out by Connie's paddock.

Josie waved bye to her mother as her father drove toward Lonsdale. She was so excited. The fair day was finally here!

A couple more turns, and they were pulling into the driveway to Lonsdale. The whole place was swarming with people. Lynne was standing on the grass in the middle of the barnyard, calling out instructions to the various riders. Josie could see Sam picking out Marmalade's hooves, and Jill was braiding Faith's mane.

"Josie!" Jill cried when she saw her. "You've got to take a look at the back."

Josie walked over to the gate that led into the fields. A smile crossed her face as she saw what was in front of her. The hedges were decorated with paper flowers, and people were working hard on all sorts of details. There was a food station, an arts-and-crafts area, and, of course, the ring where the horses and riders would be presented.

"Smells good, huh?" Anna appeared at her shoulder. "Those medieval treats smell delicious. Toffee apples, marshmallows on sticks, candy floss . . . all sorts of things."

"Sounds yummy," Josie agreed. "This is going to be an amazing fair."

People were warming up their musical instruments and there was a great sense of excitement in the air. Josie couldn't believe the amount of time and effort that had been put into the day. She watched her father hurry across the field, carrying a clipboard. A group of people gathered around him. He'd been really busy over the last couple of weeks preparing lots of different medieval games, but he'd been careful to keep it all a surprise.

Josie wondered what he had in store for them.

She turned and made her way back into the stables where she saw Ben and Tubber.

"Morning, Ben . . . hello, Tubber." She stopped to pat the skewbald gelding.

Someone had already brought Charity in from the fields, and Josie could see her horse, standing in the shade of her stall, looking relaxed. Josie drew back the door and stepped inside. "Hello, Charity," she murmured. Charity whickered softly and Josie smiled. Not only was the fair that afternoon, but Charity would be coming home with her later. Now that Faith was better, Jill would be riding her from now on. This was turning out to be a perfect day.

Humming to herself, Josie set to work grooming her horse. It wasn't long before the mare was shining like pewter, her tail flowing like spun silver.

"Ten minutes, everyone," Josie heard Sally call. "I want you in costume, then let's get into line."

Josie headed into the tack room where the costumes were hanging. She had to squeeze past a crowd of kids looking at the notice on the door which showed their positions. But Josie didn't need to look at that—after all, she and Jill were going to be taking the lead. She couldn't wait!

As she scrambled into her costume, Josie heard her mother's voice outside. She peered out of the window. A trailer was coming up the drive.

Josie rushed out in her king costume, just in time to see Hope led down the ramp. The gray mare let out a whinny of excitement as she arrived at the bottom and looked around the yard. She was surrounded on all sides by the children from Friendship House, but Hope, patient as ever, didn't seem to mind. She had bright ribbons braided into her mane, and she looked the picture of contentment as she snuffled at the children. Josie walked over to give her a pat and was welcomed with a warm nicker.

The driver of the trailer carefully guided a small wooden cart down the ramp behind Hope.

"Okay, everyone." Lynne smiled at the children, who were dressed in traditional peasant costumes of smock dresses, leggings, and tunics. "Stand back while Hope is put in the shafts, then be ready to get into the back of the cart."

"Doesn't she look great?" Mrs. Grace said. She

stood beside Josie with tears of pride welling up in her eyes.

"C'mon, Mom," Josie teased. "Get ready, or you'll make me all weepy."

Her mom gave Josie a squeeze and then went inside to get ready.

Josie went to get Charity. She led her horse out and climbed onto the saddle, adjusting her riding hat under her golden crown. Perfect. She turned to see Ben and Anna in their knight costumes, leading Tubber and Skylark over. They were carrying things that looked like rugs. "What are those for?" Josie asked, puzzled.

"They go on Tubber and Skylark," Ben explained. "To make them look like chargers."

Josie's eyes widened as she watched them roll the blankets over the horses. They even had a hood with the eyes cut out so Skylark and Tubber could see properly. Tubber's blanket was blue with little crosses all over it, and Skylark's was red with little shields. "Where did you get those?" she asked.

"Your dad found them in the school prop closet," Ben said, grinning.

Now everyone had gathered in a group. Josie

looked around her as horses jostled for position. Then Jill rode around the corner on Faith, wearing a lovely, long gown and a golden crown. Everyone gasped.

"So, how do I look?" she asked Josie.

"Beautiful!" Josie told her, grinning from ear to ear.

"Welcome to Lonsdale's first medieval fair!" Jack Harvey called out over the microphone. There was applause and cheers.

"We're ready to begin," Sally said to all the performers. "Remember to stay in order and smile!"

Everyone nodded.

Josie looked out on all the people gathered around the ring. Then she looked over at the podium that had been set up on the right-hand side of the field. Jack was there announcing to the crowd. And he was talking about Jill and Josie!

They walked forward and the crowd gasped as the procession started around the field. Josie looked across at Jill, who looked like the perfect queen, in her long, dark green gown that flowed elegantly over the sidesaddle. Josie noticed a couple pointing at Jill and Faith with admiring glances.

Josie couldn't have been happier. Charity was

beneath her, Faith was at her side, and, as she twisted around in the saddle, she could see Hope bringing up the rear, the kids from Friendship House waving and cheering from the cart.

Out of the corner of her eye, Josie saw that the games had started and apple bobbing and fencing competitions were taking place on the outskirts of the field. And a team of jugglers stood at the side, throwing brightly colored balls into the air.

"The jugglers are from your dad's drama class," Jill called across. "He's been practicing with them for weeks."

"Everyone knew about it except me?" Josie said.

"I think he wanted it to be a surprise," Jill admitted with a grin.

They completed the loop and Josie felt a bit of disappointment. "It's over," she said, sadly.

"No, it's not!" cried Jill. "Come on, the mounted games are about to start."

Josie took a look around her and saw that the parade was heading for the next field where Sally was waiting. "Do you think we should take our costumes off?" she asked.

"We don't have time for that," said Jill.

When they reached the mounted games area, they grabbed a number from the organizer and arranged themselves into teams.

Josie turned to see Marmalade and Sam canter over to the area. Josie couldn't believe the change that had come over the horse now that he had Sam's full attention. He was acting like an angel.

Jill stayed with Faith as the others tried to complete the obstacles. Faith wasn't up to participating. And Jill was happy to cheer her friends on from the fence. There were speed-weaver competitions, where the riders had to turn in and out of the poles along the length of the field. Then they played flag flyers where they had to pick the flags out of a small container and deposit them in another. And finally, the game that Josie liked most, the sword lancers—where you held a pole and collected little rings from the tops of cones with a wooden sword. As they galloped along, Josie felt like a real medieval knight!

"You were great!" Jill told her friends.

"Thanks," Josie said.

"Let's give the horses a rest," Jill said. "I think that they deserve it."

"Good idea," said Josie. "Besides, I want to play some of the other games," she added, pointing out the rest of the activities around the fields.

"Definitely that one," Jill laughed, nodding in the direction of Amelia, who was sitting in some stocks being pelted with sodden sponges by her friends.

"For sure!" Josie agreed. "Come on, let's go!"

The fair was a huge success. Everyone had a great time—and a lot of money was raised for Friendship House. At the end of the day all the Graces, the Marshalls, and Jill helped Sally count up the money.

"Thank you all for helping," Sally told everyone.

Anna, Jill, and Josie went out to the stalls to see their horses. As Josie walked along, she linked arms with her best friend and her newest friend. The School Farm horses were out in the paddock together. Faith, Hope, and Charity were together again, grazing happily. Yes, Josie sighed. This was a perfect fair, and a perfect day.